MELTDOWN

GRACEMOUNT

LIE

SPECIAL AGENTS

Also in the **SPECIAL AGENTS** series:

22460

SPECIAL AGENTS
MELTDOWN

sam hutton

With special thanks to Allan Frewin Jones

Thanks also to Kath Jatter

HarperCollins *Children's Books*

First published in Great Britain by HarperCollins *Children's Books* 2005
HarperCollins *Children's Books* is a division of HarperCollins*Publishers* Ltd
77-85 Fulham Palace Road, Hammersmith, London W6 8JB

The HarperCollins *Children's Books* website address is
www.harpercollinschildrensbooks.co.uk

2

ISBN-10   0 00 714847 X
ISBN-13   978 0 00 714847 9

Text and series concept © Working Partners Limited 2005
Chapter illustrations by Tim Stevens

Printed and bound in England by Clays Ltd, St Ives plc

Conditions of Sale

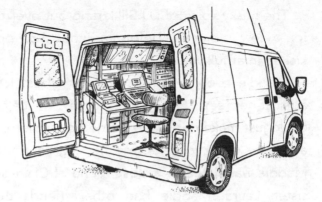

Prologue

London.

A nightclub called Cloud Nine.

Monday night.

Maddie Cooper leant over the balcony, watching the coloured lights as they wheeled and strobed over the party goers below. The music never stopped – the Turbosound loudspeakers pounding out exhilarating, relentless rhythms. The dance floor was seething, but there was a chill-out lounge up on the balcony with large leather sofas. Maddie had been dancing most of the night – now she needed an iced Coke and a chance to catch her breath.

The husky voice of DJ Slikk rang out over the music for a few moments before another 120 bpm track kicked in at full volume.

Maddie took a drink from her glass. Ice rattled against her teeth. She smiled, sucking an ice cube. She could just make out Claire Petrie down there. This was a private party to celebrate her eighteenth birthday. Maddie was sixteen – a close friend of Claire's younger sister, Laura. Maddie had other friends there too: Susannah – Jules – Deborah – Alice. Fellow students from her days at the White Lodge Ballet School.

Maddie was having a great time, meeting all her old friends again – she hadn't seen some of them for over twelve months. Not since the night last July that had changed her life for ever. It was good to catch up.

Her smile faded as she watched one particular girl. A friend of a friend. Her name was Zoë – that was all Maddie knew about her. She was small and slim, with long blonde hair and large, pale blue eyes.

Maddie's gaze followed her as she raced across the lounge area. There was something about the way Zoë was behaving that didn't seem natural. It was almost as if she was high on something. But that wasn't possible – the party was strictly drugs-free.

"Hey, Maddie!"

"Hey, Susannah." Maddie smiled at her old friend.

"Isn't this great?" Susannah said. "There must be three hundred people here."

Maddie laughed. "At least." She looked around and found herself staring at one boy in particular. Tall, good-looking. He was leaning over the balcony, watching the dancers. "Do you know him?" Maddie asked, nodding towards the boy.

Susannah shrugged. "No. Never seen him before. Maybe he's a friend of Claire's." She grinned. "Do you want me to go over and tell him you like him?"

"I can do that myself, thanks very much," said Maddie. She arched an eyebrow. "He's quite cute, isn't he?"

The boy chose that moment suddenly to lift his head. Maddie found herself looking straight into his eyes. He smiled. Slightly embarrassed to be caught staring at him, she smiled back, then turned away.

"He's coming over," said Susannah. "I think you've scored, Maddie."

Maddie laughed. "Grow up, Susannah."

"I'll leave you to it," Susannah said. "But you've got to promise to report back to me later."

The young man circled the balcony and came to stand in front of her. He didn't speak. Maddie looked at

7

him. He had grey eyes and dark brown hair.

"Hi," she said.

"I know this place is called Cloud Nine," he said, "but I didn't expect to meet an angel."

She gave him a look of amused disbelief. "You've got to be kidding me?"

He smiled sheepishly. "It sounded really good when I was practising it," he said.

"Keep practising," Maddie said with a smile. "I'm sure you'll come up with something that works – eventually. I'm Maddie."

"Paul," he said. "I noticed you – on the dance floor. You're a great dancer."

"Thank you."

"Maybe you should take it up professionally," he suggested.

She shook her head. "Not an option," she said.

"No? Why's that?"

Maddie felt it was time for a change of subject. "Where do you know Claire from?"

He hesitated. "Oh – around. You know."

She looked keenly at him. "You don't know her at all, do you?"

He gave her a weak grin. "Promise not to tell anyone – but I wasn't actually invited. I tagged along with some friends." He looked straight into her eyes. "You know something, Maddie – you'd make a good detective."

"You think?" Maddie said with a wry smile. "The dancing detective – that's kind of catchy."

"So – are you going to have me thrown out?" he asked.

She shook her head. "I don't think so. Not right this minute, anyway."

He smiled. "You see – I was right – you are an angel."

They chatted easily. Paul plied her with questions about herself – she offered friendly answers that didn't give too much away. There were things in her past that she wasn't prepared to offer up in party small talk.

Maddie liked him, but something made her just a little bit wary. He didn't always keep eye contact. He didn't give very much away about himself. Maybe it was just nervousness, she decided. He was very cute – and he seemed to be genuinely interested in her.

She thought she'd take a chance on him. "Would you like to swap phone numbers?" she said. "Maybe we could meet up again some time?" She took her mobile out of her shoulder bag. "Do you have a phone on you?" she asked.

He drew out a slimline phone. She took it from him,

switched it on and programmed her own number into it. He took hers and did the same.

They had only just handed their phones back when someone lurched into Maddie's back and she was thrown forwards into Paul's arms.

"Sorry... sorry..." said a voice. Maddie looked around. It was Zoë. Her face was red – dripping with sweat. She seemed to be having trouble keeping her balance.

"Are you OK?" Maddie asked her.

Zoë grabbed at Paul. "I feel strange," she said, her voice slurred and shrill.

Paul fended her off. "Maybe you should go and sit down," he said awkwardly, pulling away from the girl's clutching hands. Maddie assumed from his behaviour that he had no idea who she was.

"I need to get out of here," Zoë mumbled, her arms beginning to flail. "I want to go home. I don't want to be here. I feel really ill."

Her legs suddenly buckled. Paul stepped back. Maddie reached forwards and caught hold of Zoë as she collapsed. Zoë's weight dragged her down. Her skin was hot and damp. She tried to speak, but suddenly she was limp in Maddie's arms.

Maddie turned Zoë on to her back. The girl's eyes

were closed. Her mouth hung open. Sweat was pouring off her.

Maddie tapped her cheek. "Zoë? Are you OK?"

There was no response.

She looked up at Paul. "Call 999," she said. "She's unconscious."

People were gathering around now. Maddie ignored them.

She lifted one of Zoë's eyelids. The pupil was dilated. She slid a hand under Zoë's neck and tilted her head back, checking that her airway was clear. She pressed her fingers to the artery in the girl's neck. The pulse was strong and steady. That was good. Zoë didn't seem to be in immediate danger.

Maddie put her in the recovery position – on her side with one arm and one leg drawn up to support her body.

Susannah was one of the people crowding round. "What happened?" she asked.

"I don't know," Maddie said. "I thought there was something peculiar about the way she was acting when I saw her earlier – but now she's completely out of it."

Others gathered close. Paul crouched at Maddie's side. She felt his hand resting on her back. His mouth came close to her ear.

11

"I like you," he whispered. "I'm really sorry about this."

She looked around – puzzled. What did he mean? He was already standing up. He stepped back into the ring of anxious faces.

"I don't believe this!" It was Claire's voice. "What's going on?"

Maddie explained again.

"Oh great," Claire said. "Way to ruin my party, Zoë!"

Maddie looked up at her. "I don't think she did this on purpose," she said. She stood up and looked around for Paul. She couldn't see him.

The crowd parted.

"We're police officers," said a voice. "Step away, please."

Maddie looked in surprise at the two plain-clothed men. One of them showed her a CID identity card. Someone had obviously alerted them to the incident – but they must have been very close by to have arrived so quickly.

"She's unconscious," Maddie said. "I've checked her out – she should be fine till an ambulance gets here."

One of the men knelt at Zoë's side. The other looked at Maddie.

"And you would be?" he asked.

"Maddie Cooper," she said.

The police officer nodded, as if she had confirmed something for him. "Would you mind turning out the contents of your bag, please, Miss Cooper?" he said.

Maddie stared at him in surprise. "Excuse me?" she said.

"The bag," he said, pointing. "Now, please."

Maddie pulled her shoulder bag around and opened it. She reached into it. Something unexpected met her fingers. She withdrew her hand – confused. She was holding a roll of twenty-pound notes. There had to be several hundred pounds there. It wasn't her money. She had no idea where it could have come from.

The policeman took the roll of banknotes. In a daze, Maddie reached into the bag again. Her hand came out. There was a small plastic bag. It had twenty or so little pink pills in it. Each of them was indented with the letter G.

Her head spun. She recognised the pills – they were illegal drugs – amphetamines.

The policeman took the plastic bag from her.

"These look like Gems to me, miss," he said.

Maddie was stunned. "I don't know how they got there," she said, acutely aware of how lame it sounded.

The policeman put his hand on her arm. "I am

arresting you for possession of a suspected Class A drug. You do not have to say anything, but it may harm your defence if you do not mention when questioned something which you later rely on in court. Anything you do say may be given in evidence."

Maddie was too shocked to speak. She could feel the eyes of 300 people following her as the two policemen led her down to ground level and out into the cool September night.

This wasn't happening to her. It couldn't be real.

Chapter One

PIC Control.

The Centre Point building, London.

05:37.

The lift doors opened and nineteen-year-old Alex Cox stepped into the long, brightly lit open-plan office. Even at this time in the morning, the Police Investigation Command headquarters buzzed with activity.

A call from Danny Bell had brought Alex in three hours before his shift was due to start.

Alex nodded a greeting to Jackie Saunders, the Communications Officer. She barely acknowledged him. He frowned – this wasn't the first time recently that he had noticed a change in her behaviour. But he had no time to worry about that now. He headed straight over to Danny's work station.

Danny was sitting on the desk with his feet on the chair – speaking on the phone. He was a black American, a year younger than the Londoner, Alex. Born and bred in Chicago, he had come to the UK with his father on an FBI witness-relocation programme. He never discussed it, but Alex knew that Danny's father had testified against the Mob. Their only hope of avoiding reprisals had been to leave America for good.

Danny and Alex had been recruited to this elite branch of the Metropolitan Police at more or less the same time – hand-picked by the boss, despite their youth, they were two of the three fast-track trainees on PIC's payroll.

Alex's concern that morning was for the third trainee: PIC agent Maddie Cooper.

Danny had been on the graveyard shift when the news had come through: Agent Cooper had been picked up by two police officers from the Charing Cross branch – arrested for the possession of illegal drugs.

Danny finished his call and put the phone down.

"Maddie with drugs?" Alex said incredulously to his

colleague. "Is someone having a laugh?"

Danny shook his head. "They think she was pushing Gems," he said. "They found twenty-six of them on her. And a wad of twenty-pound notes."

"No way," Alex said. "This is crazy. Have you spoken to her?"

"No. The boss is with her. He's taken her home. She's been bailed to return in ten days – pending chemical analysis of the pills." He frowned. "I just spoke to someone over at the station. They're pretty sure the pills are Gems."

Alex took out his mobile phone and scrolled for a number.

"What are you doing?" Danny asked.

"I'm going to call her," Alex said. "This has got to be sorted."

Danny raised his eyebrows. "She's been up all night, Alex. Give her a break – she'll be dead on her feet."

"How come they picked on her?"

"Beats me." Danny looked at his colleague. "All I know is that she had the pills on her – and that she was carrying a roll of notes that looked like a dealer's bundle."

"This stinks," Alex said.

Danny nodded. "It sure does. But as far as those

guys down at Charing Cross are concerned, she was found in possession. End of story. They've got to play it by the book." He shook his head. "This isn't going to fade away, Alex. Maddie could be in some serious trouble."

✲

For Maddie, the past few hours had been like a nightmare.

The journey to the police station.

The wait for her father to arrive with the duty solicitor.

The interview.

The utter disbelief that this was really happening to her.

Her father's rock-solid faith in her innocence helped her get through the ordeal, but she still fell into her gran's arms when she got home – drained, exhausted and bewildered.

The three of them sat at the kitchen table.

Jack Cooper leant forward in his wheelchair, frowning as he spoke. "Have you remembered *anything* that you didn't tell the interviewing officer? Something trivial, maybe. Something that seemed totally ordinary at the time, but which might give us a clue as to how the drugs and the money got into your bag." His eyes burnt with determination. "Think, Maddie."

She shuddered. "I am thinking," she said quietly.

Her gran frowned at him. "Gently, Jack."

Jack Cooper patted his daughter's hand. "I'm sorry," he said. "The last thing you need right now is to be badgered by me."

Maddie shook her head. "No, it's fine, Dad. I understand." She held tightly on to her gran's hand. "It's like I told them at the station. I had the bag with me all the time. I suppose someone could have slipped the stuff in there while I was dancing – but I don't think that's what happened."

"You believe it was the boy who called himself Paul?" her father said.

Maddie frowned. "I think it must have been. It would make sense of what he said. Zoë was down – I was making sure she was OK. He knelt beside me. He said, 'I'm sorry – I really like you.' Then he was gone." She looked at her father. "Why would he say he was sorry?"

"I don't know," Jack Cooper said. "But I'll make sure it's one of the first questions he's asked once he's been tracked down." His fist came down hard on the table. "They'd better pull out all the stops on this one or they'll have me to answer to."

"I think maybe you should try to get some sleep,

Maddie," said her gran. "You look exhausted."

Maddie tried a half-smile. "It's been quite a night," she said, wiping a hand across her stinging eyes. She was close to tears from the stress. She looked at her father. "Is it OK if I come in late tomorrow?" she asked. She glanced at her watch. "Today, I mean." It was gone half-six in the morning – beyond the kitchen blinds the city was already waking up.

The expression on her father's face disturbed her. It was a look of concern and distress.

"What's wrong?" she whispered.

"Listen, Maddie – there's no easy way for me to tell you this. You'll have to be suspended from duties until this mess has been cleared up."

"But I haven't done anything wrong," Maddie said.

"I know," said her father. "But those are the rules. You're an officer in the Metropolitan Police, Maddie. As such, you have to aspire to the highest possible standards. We all do. Any officer suspected of being involved in criminal activities has to be suspended pending a full investigation. That's the way it works. I can't bend the rules – not even for my own daughter."

Maddie swallowed hard. "How long does this kind of thing usually take?" she asked.

"Don't worry about that right now," said her father.

He looked at his watch. "I'll give Tara a ring. She can come and pick me up. I'm not going to be able to sleep now and there are a few phone calls I can make to get things moving along."

Maddie's mouth was dry. "This is serious, isn't it?" she said softly.

He looked into her eyes for a few heavy moments.

"Yes," he said. "It's serious. You should try to get some sleep now." He looked at her gran. "I'll be in touch as soon as I find out what's happening."

Maddie lay in bed, staring up at the ceiling. It felt as if the ground had fallen away from beneath her feet over the past few hours.

The previous evening she had been in control – holding down an important and fulfilling job, knowing where she was going and how she was going to get there. And now everything had changed. She was under suspicion of a serious crime and all the certainties she had come to rely on seemed to be crumbling around her.

It was a long time before exhaustion finally overwhelmed her and she fell into a shallow, fitful sleep.

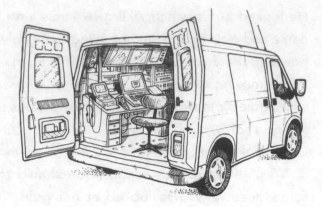

Chapter Two

PIC Control.

10:47.

Tara Moon was at her desk in the small anteroom that led to DCS Cooper's office. A lot of people wanted a piece of her boss and, as his PA, it was her job to create a buffer between him and the rest of the world. She was also his chauffeur and minder, so she was used to working long hours – and being called from her bed in the middle of the night to help Jack Cooper deal with a sudden crisis.

The arrest of Jack Cooper's daughter had sent shock waves through the elite police team. One of their own was in trouble and for once there was little that PIC could do about it.

There would be a major briefing soon – in the meantime, Tara worked on some financial spreadsheets on her computer, transferring funds to various Section Heads and double-checking the allocation of resources within the department.

A new Home Secretary had taken office – a formidable woman called Margaret Churchill. She had come to the job with a manifesto to reduce costs across the board. Tara had to ensure that PIC's finances showed no irregularities. It was a task at which she excelled.

The intercom sounded. "Tara. In here, please."

Tara saved her work and went into Jack Cooper's office. PIC Control was at the top of the Centre Point tower. Behind her boss's desk, broad windows overlooked a panorama of London: the Houses of Parliament, the River Thames and the London Eye.

Tara stood to attention at Jack Cooper's desk. He was studying some documents that had been biked over by a Home Office courier. The envelope had been marked A1X clearance only – not to be viewed by anyone other than DCS Cooper himself.

He looked up at her. "I've had instructions to allow

full access to..." He hesitated for a moment. "To an outsider. She will be working here on a special project for the next few days. You are to help her in any way that she asks."

"May I ask the nature of this special project, sir?" she asked.

Jack Cooper looked down at the documents. "No. You may not."

"Thank you, sir." Tara turned on her heel and strode to the door.

"Tara."

She looked back.

"This is one time when you don't need to know," Cooper said. "Understood?"

"Understood, sir."

Tara closed the door and returned thoughtfully to her desk. For a few moments she stared into space, then she turned back to her computer and continued to work.

❂

The Briefing Room.

11:03.

Jack Cooper sat at the head of the room. Unusually, Tara was missing from his side – she had other duties to perform that morning. Around DCS Cooper were gathered all the available PIC Section Heads, along with a select group of field agents. Maddie's closest colleagues were also there – Danny and Alex, sitting together, eager for news.

Each agent had their own computer terminal and there was a large digital screen on the wall directly behind Jack Cooper. Morning briefings like this were routine, but the agenda had been revised to include an unusual and disturbing item: the arrest of Madeleine Cooper.

"Is it possible that Maddie's problem has anything to do with Operation Flatline?" asked Kevin Randal. "Maybe we're ruffling a few feathers and they've decided to play some dirty tricks to distract our attention?"

Operation Flatline: a long-term war on the gangs involved in London's drugs trade, specifically targeting the manufacturers and distributors of a new drug known on the streets as Gems. PIC agents had been working on this for a couple of months and there was a belief in Kevin Randal's undercover team that they were getting close to something important.

"Would someone like to explain Gems to those of you who are new to Operation Flatline?" Cooper said.

Danny spoke up. "Gems are a brand-new type of amphetamine," he explained. "They come in the form of small pink pills. They dissolve in water, leaving no taste or smell. The word on the street is that they're a mild, good-time recreational drug – but there's a whole lot more to them than having a great night out. The chemical breakdown shows that Gems contain a powerful serotonin stripper – a chemical which attacks 5-hydroxytryptamine. It has the effect of hitting a user with a massive rush of paranoia." He looked around the room. "These little pink pills have a nasty sting in the tail."

"The pills found on Maddie have been taken away for chemical analysis," said Cooper. "But the officer in charge of her arrest is convinced that they're the genuine article." He leant forwards in his wheelchair. "It turns out that Charing Cross police station received an anonymous phone call last night, recommending that they send a squad car over to Cloud Nine to pick up a drugs dealer who was working the club." His voice rumbled dangerously. "They were given my daughter's name."

Alex and Danny looked at one another. A tip-off putting the finger on Maddie. What was going on?

"The questions we need to concentrate on are these," Jack Cooper continued. "Who made that call – and why was my daughter targeted?"

Maddie still felt dazed. The few brief hours of shallow sleep that she had snatched had left her desperately weary. As she ascended in the Centre Point lift, she wondered how her colleagues would treat her. She hoped they wouldn't be too sympathetic – she was just managing to hold it together and a wave of sympathy would just about finish her off.

The lift doors opened. Maddie stepped out into the busy office. Jackie Saunders was on the phone. She glanced at Maddie then looked away. No smile. Nothing. Odd.

Maddie walked straight to her desk. Her plan was to be in and out of there as quickly as possible. She didn't want to draw attention to herself while she sorted out the few things that could not be left till her return – whenever that might be.

She sat at her work station and booted up her computer. Some urgent files needed to be transferred to other agents. Once that had been done, she would have nothing else to do other than to go home and wait for the nightmare to end.

The revelation that Maddie had been specifically named as a suspected drugs dealer had changed the nature of the briefing. It now looked as though PIC itself was under attack.

"We can rule out the idea that the boy calling himself Paul acted randomly or dumped the drugs on Maddie out of panic," Jack Cooper was saying. "She was deliberately set up. DCI Randal has suggested that this may be connected with Operation Flatline and I'm inclined to agree with him. Therefore, we should be concentrating our efforts on tracking down the big dealers – the guys behind closed doors."

"Surely our number-one priority should be clearing Maddie?" Alex said. "Has anyone been sent over to Cloud Nine to talk to the staff? Do we have a list of the people at the party? We could doorstep them. Someone there must have known who this Paul guy was."

Jack Cooper's face was expressionless as he looked at Alex. "Those kind of enquiries will be dealt with by the arresting officers. We'll be told as soon as they have any further information. In the meantime, we concentrate on our own job."

"And what happens to Maddie?" Danny asked.

"I've suspended her," said Jack Cooper. "She'll have to sit tight and wait for the enquiry to run its course – just like any of us would."

Danny stared at him. "You're putting me on! Don't

those guys over at Charing Cross know who she is? Can't you call in a few favours, boss – you know – to make this thing go away?"

Jack Cooper looked steadily at him. "What are you suggesting, Danny? That I call up the Deputy Assistant Commissioner of the City of Westminster Borough Operational Command Unit and tell him to drop the case because Maddie is my daughter?"

Danny looked at him. "Uh... yes, kind of. I guess."

"That's not an option. And you know it."

Danny winced under Jack Cooper's fierce gaze. "Yes, OK. I know. But it's Maddie, right? We've got to do *something*."

"Someone should go and speak to Zoë Baker," Alex suggested.

"As far as I know, Zoë Baker is still unconscious in hospital," said Cooper. "When she's able to give a statement it will be taken by the borough CID. Obviously our hope is that she'll point the finger at Paul. Maybe she knows him. Maybe she got him into the party. Maybe she can lead us straight to him." He paused, frowning. "That's a lot of maybes. If Zoë Baker just turns out to be someone who got caught up in the wheels, then the line of enquiry will have to be widened to include the nightclub staff and other party guests.

But those enquiries will be run from Charing Cross – not from here."

"Was Maddie able to give them anything useful about Paul?" Section Head DCI Susan Baxendale asked.

"Nothing I haven't already told you," Jack Cooper said. "She gave the officers at Charing Cross a description of his appearance – but that's about it. She didn't find out anything else about him. They exchanged mobile numbers but the number Paul gave her doesn't exist."

"Do we know where the call targeting Maddie came from?" Alex asked.

"It was made on a public phone in Hammersmith," Jack Cooper said. "The caller was male, but it wasn't Paul – he was already at the party when the call was made."

"So he definitely had an accomplice," Susan Baxendale said.

"That's right," said Cooper. "And my guess is that the man who made that call is also the man who set my daughter up."

"That would make sense," said Kevin Randal. "He sends Paul in to do the legwork while he keeps out of sight. Smart guy."

"We need to find that man," Jack Cooper said. "I've a gut feeling that if we get him, we also get the Gems factory." His voice lowered to an angry murmur. "I plan on making that man sorry he ever chose to use Maddie as a way of getting at us."

☻

Maddie transferred the final file. She sat gazing at her screen for a few moments before clicking to exit the computer. She was suddenly aware of someone standing behind her.

She looked around. It was Tara.

"I've finished," Maddie said dully. "I'm just going to close down and then I'll be out of here." She sighed and ran her fingers through her hair. "Thanks for coming over, but I'm fine."

Tara looked at her. "I'm glad to hear it," she said. "But I'm not here to see how you are, Maddie. I need your pass."

"Oh – yes – sorry." Maddie took out her PIC ID card and handed it to Tara. "At least I still know all the security codes," she said with a weak smile.

Tara shook her head. "Not any more you don't. They were changed this morning."

She slipped Maddie's ID card into a plastic folder and walked away without another word.

Maddie sat at her desk. Stunned. The reality of her situation finally hit home. She had been locked out of PIC Control.

She was out in the cold.

Chapter Three

PIC Control.

The Briefing Room.

The briefing had moved on to practical matters.

Jack Cooper was reading from an external report. "Our colleagues in Special Branch have allowed us access to some of their files," he told his team. "They make for interesting reading. Over the past few months, Special Branch drugs swoops have netted plenty of people caught dealing Gems." He looked around the room. "All small fry, unfortunately – street peddlers. These aren't the people we need. We have to get to the suppliers higher up the chain – the people who can lead us to where the pills are being manufactured."

He pressed some keys and a map of southeast England appeared on each computer screen. The map was scattered with red dots.

"This shows where Gems have turned up in the past two months," said Cooper. "The pattern forms a circle – and London's right in the middle. These drugs are being made here – most likely in a factory unit. We need to close that factory down. Kevin – how many agents can you put on the streets?"

"Twelve if I drop everything else," said Kevin Randal.

"I can release another six," said Susan Baxendale.

"Do it," said Cooper. "Operation Flatline has just become our number-one priority. These people have got to be stopped."

Danny lifted his hand. "I've been working a guy over in Camden," he said. "A pusher called Harvey Silver. He's been dropping hints about a big-time dealer in that area. I've been playing it cool so far, but maybe I should put some heat under him and see what sweats out."

"Do that," said Cooper. "Find out what he knows. If the information looks good, try to arrange a meet with the other man. We need access to some big players – and we need it now."

Maddie stepped out on to the paved forecourt of Centre Point. The streets were loud and busy. Cars and buses nosed their way up and down Charing Cross Road. Pedestrians filled the pavements.

Maddie heaved her bag on to her shoulder. She had taken a few personal items away with her. Her work station had looked strangely empty as she had walked away. She had a bad feeling in the pit of her stomach that it would be some time before she sat there again.

She walked towards the steps down to the Underground. Everything around her hummed with purpose and energy – places to go – people to see – work to be done.

Maddie stood in the middle of all this activity with a long, blank day stretching out ahead of her.

She turned and looked up. The massive glass and concrete tower of Centre Point reared above her. She felt as though she had left the focus of her life up there.

Maddie turned and walked slowly down the steps, before she was swallowed by the crowd.

✪

The Briefing Room had cleared. Jack Cooper pressed Exit on his keyboard and the networked computers went into standby mode. He sat there for a few moments, watching the endless forward flow of screensaver stars.

His thoughts were interrupted by a sound from the doorway.

Danny and Alex were standing there. "Could we have a word, boss?" Alex asked.

He nodded. They came back into the room.

"Alex and I have been talking it over," Danny said.

"Maddie, Danny and I have always worked as a team, boss," Alex said. "We have to get her off the hook."

"The thing is," Danny added. "We think there's a better way for us to help Maddie than just rounding up all the usual suspects and pumping them for the address of the Gems factory."

Jack Cooper eyed them. "You have a plan?" he said.

"We need to talk to Zoë Baker," Alex replied. "Send us over to the Chelsea and Westminster Hospital. We'll get her side of the story."

"She could lead us to Paul," Danny added. "Paul will lead us to the man on the phone – and he'll lead us to the people who are cranking out the Gems. We'll be able to prove that Maddie was set up and we'll blow the Gems factory out of the water all in one big hit." He looked at his boss. "What do you say – is it a go?"

Jack Cooper looked at them for a few moments. "Let me make this perfectly clear," he sighed. "The investigation into Maddie's arrest is being pursued by officers of Charing Cross police station. There are no circumstances under which any agent of PIC is to become involved. You are not to approach any potential witnesses – and you will not try to get a statement from Zoë Baker. Is that understood?"

"Yes, boss," said Alex.

Jack Cooper wheeled himself past them. He paused, looking back. "I know you're trying to help, but keep away from that hospital. And that's an order."

Danny lifted his hand to the side of his head in a kind of half-salute. "You got it, boss. The Chelsea and Westminster Hospital is a no-go area."

The door closed behind Jack Cooper.

Danny and Alex looked at one another.

Danny raised an eyebrow.

Alex nodded.

Message received and understood.

Chapter Four

The Chelsea and Westminster Hospital.

Fulham Road, SW10.

13:22.

Alex and Danny walked in through a set of wide revolving doors. The building was ultramodern – glass, steel and high white walls hung with splashes of modern art. The ground floor atrium soared up thirty metres, creating a huge space, filled with light and glowing with vibrant, shifting colours.

Alex was carrying a bunch of flowers in his arms. Danny had a fruit basket. They approached the curved reception desk.

A young woman smiled enquiringly.

"A friend of ours was admitted last night," Danny said. "Zoë Baker. We don't know which ward she's in."

"Just a moment." The young woman tapped at a keyboard. "She's in Elizabeth Gaskell ward. Second floor."

Danny plucked a white rose from the bunch that Alex was carrying. Smiling, he handed it to the young woman.

"Thank you!" she laughed in surprise. "Go to lift bank B. That'll take you up to the ward."

They walked through into the towering, airy hospital. Escalators tracked up and down. A large chrome cube ran with glistening water. There was a huge red, yellow and green steel sculpture – The Acrobat. A mobile of rainbow-coloured leaves fluttered down the full five floors from the transparent plastic roof.

"This place is more like an art gallery than a hospital," Alex said. "I hope they bring me here if I ever get ill!"

They stepped into a gleaming metal lift.

A few smooth moments later, the doors opened and they made their way to the ward.

"Notice something else?" Danny said. "It doesn't even smell like a hospital."

The ward had a reception area and doors leading to small side rooms.

A man with cropped bleached hair was working at the desk.

Danny explained the reason for their visit.

"Zoë?" said the young man. He pointed. "We've put her in a side room. She's sleeping. We're not allowing her any visitors at the moment."

Alex looked at him. "Sleeping? Not unconscious?"

"She came out of it in the middle of the night," said the bleach-haired man. "The overdose wasn't as bad as we'd feared."

"So what happened when she got here?" Danny asked.

"We went into the usual emergency routine," the man said. "We emptied out her stomach and aspirated her to get rid of any bits and pieces. Then we gave her some activated charcoal to mop up the remnants. She was out of it for a couple of hours after that. When she woke up she was disorientated and a little bit distressed, so we gave her a mild sedative."

"But she's in no danger?" asked Danny.

"The test results aren't back yet," said the man. "We can't be sure what's going on until we've got a better idea of what she took." He smiled reassuringly. "The chances are we got to her in time. She was lucky."

"How soon is she likely to wake up?" Alex asked.

"It could be any time now," said the man. "You're welcome to wait." He gestured towards a doorway. "We're expecting her parents at any moment. They're driving down from a holiday in Scotland. Do you know them?"

"I'm afraid not," Alex said.

"There are a couple of other people waiting already," the man said. "You could sit with them."

"Friends?" Alex asked.

"I don't think so," said the man. "Police, I think."

Danny and Alex exchanged a glance.

"We'll come back later," Danny said. "Could you give her these?" He placed the fruit basket on the desk. Alex laid the flowers alongside.

The man nodded. "Who shall I say they're from?" he asked.

"Tell her they're from her best mates," said Danny. "She'll know who you mean."

Alex glanced quickly into the waiting room as they left the ward. A man and a woman were sitting there reading magazines. CID. Definitely.

The risk that they would be recognised by these officers was minimal, but the police presence at the hospital would make having a quiet word with Zoë a little tricky.

"Now what?" Alex asked as they descended in the lift.

"Plan B," said Danny.

"I didn't know there was a Plan B."

Danny smiled. "There's always a Plan B."

❂

The Mobile Surveillance Unit was parked in a side street. From the outside, it looked like an ordinary white van – but it was packed with state-of-the-art electronics.

Danny disengaged the high-security alarm system and climbed into the back. He emerged a minute later. He stepped down on to the road and opened his hand.

Alex nodded. Now he understood Danny's Plan B.

Displayed on Danny's palm was a miniature UHF transmitter.

"This little baby will pick up an ant whispering secrets at fifteen metres," Danny said proudly. "It'll transmit to the MSU scanner. We'll be able to hear every word in that room, clear as crystal. We just sit back and wait for our friends from Charing Cross to go in there and ask the questions." He grinned. "Job done."

"How do we get it in there?" Alex asked. "Maybe

we should have hidden that bug in the fruit or flowers."

"Too obvious," Danny replied. "It's always possible the police would check for something like that. No, this is better. We simply dress up as regular hospital staff and hope for the best. I can act the part of a brilliant young neurosurgeon." He looked at Alex. "You can be a trainee nurse."

Alex looked back at him. "How about I'm the brain surgeon and you're my most challenging patient?"

"That could work," Danny said. "But it's probably best if we keep it low-key."

"We should look out for coats – that would make us look like orderlies or porters," Alex said.

Danny nodded.

They re-entered the hospital, this time taking the escalator up to the ward. They avoided the main entrance, searching the corridors and hallways, moving purposefully, always keeping up the appearance of knowing exactly where they were going.

They found a staff changing room and pulled on orderlies' coats. Then they discovered a back way on to the ward – a flight of stairs which led to a sun lounge where patients could sit and watch television.

"It's showtime," Danny said.

They walked on to Elizabeth Gaskell ward.

A nurse approached them. "Who are you?" she asked.

"The agency sent us," Danny replied. "We were told to come up here and make ourselves useful."

"You can't just wander around," she said. "Go and speak to the ward sister. She'll assign you some duties."

"Thanks, we'll do that," Danny said.

Alex spotted a store room with an open door. He ducked out of sight for a moment and came back carrying a mop and bucket.

They walked the length of the ward without anyone else questioning them.

The door to Zoë's side room was open. They slipped inside. There were four beds, but only one was occupied.

Zoë was curled up on her side.

Alex stood close to the door – ready to stall anyone who wanted to come in.

Danny moved quickly over to the bed. Zoë looked pale but peaceful.

He leant forwards, peeling the tape off the adhesive surface of the bug, intending to attach it under the metal frame near her head.

He found himself looking into a pair of pale blue eyes.

"Hi, Zoë," he said. "How's it going?"

Alex glanced around. Zoë had woken up.

"My head hurts," Zoë murmured. "So does my stomach."

"I think that's from them pumping you out, Zoë," Danny said. He smiled. "You must have had quite a night. Do you remember any of it?"

Zoë turned on to her back. Danny rearranged her pillows. Alex quietly closed the door. He kept watch through the glass panel.

"I remember acting stupid," Zoë murmured. "My mouth's dry."

Danny poured her a cup of water from a bedside jug. She drank slowly and with evident discomfort. "Do you know what made you ill?" Danny asked.

Danny knew he didn't have much time. He glanced over at Alex. Alex nodded – everything was OK so far.

"I took some pills," Zoë said. She closed her eyes. "Stupid thing to do. I've never done anything like that before."

Danny smiled. "I guess you won't do it again, either."

"Not in a million years." She opened her eyes. She looked drained and weary. "The guy who gave them to me said they'd just make me feel good. He said they were called Gems. He gave me six of them – he said they were really mild – that they'd just give me a kick, you know?"

"Some kick," said Danny.

"I thought they must be pretty harmless," Zoë said. "Otherwise he wouldn't have just handed them over like that." She swallowed some water with difficulty. "I took all six."

Danny winced. "Bad move," he said.

"Tell me about it," said Zoë. A tear ran down her face. "My mum will go insane," she whispered. "I've only been in London for three weeks. I'm down here for college."

"Don't worry about your mom," Danny said. "She'll be too relieved that you're OK to beat you up." He looked at her. "Did you know the guy who gave you the pills?"

Zoë shook her head, frowning. "His name was Paul. That's all I know. I remember he was talking with a blonde girl – I can't remember her name – she's a friend of Claire's sister."

She obviously meant Maddie. "Did you see him with anyone else?" Danny asked.

"Earlier on, before he came over to me, I saw him talking to the club DJ – Slikk. Maybe she knows him." She closed her eyes again and sank deeper into her pillows. "I'm tired. I hope the police lock him up and throw away the key."

Danny straightened up. "I'll let you sleep, Zoë," he said. He touched her shoulder. "You'll be just fine. But remember – next time a stranger offers you some pretty pills in a nightclub..."

"Just say no," Zoë interrupted with a weak smile. "Don't worry. I've learnt my lesson."

"Good," Danny said. "You could have ended up in a coma – or worse."

She nodded.

"Danny..." Alex said in a warning voice.

Someone was coming.

Danny pocketed the transmitter – he already had all the information he needed. He walked to the door and the two of them slipped out.

A man and a woman were walking towards them. They had strained, anxious faces. Zoë's parents – straight from a desperate drive down from their Scottish holiday.

Danny and Alex melted into the background.

"Right then," Danny said. "Next stop – DJ Slikk."

Chapter Five

The Coopers' flat, St John's Wood, NW8.

Mid-afternoon.

Maddie stalked the rooms like a caged animal. Her gran had gone out with some friends – a day trip to Sissinghurst Castle Gardens. Gran was mad about flowers. She wouldn't be home till the early evening. Maddie had been invited along, but couldn't face it. She'd said that she wanted to be alone. She wasn't so sure about that any more. The truth was, she didn't know what she wanted – except for this madness to be over.

Her father was at work and her friends were at college. Alex and Danny would have enough on their plates without phone calls from her. There was no one to talk to. The feeling of helplessness was driving her crazy.

She had tried reading but she hadn't been able to concentrate. Music on the radio just seemed to be laughing at her. Daytime TV was no better – smiley happy faces and good times. They grated on her and she had switched off after only a few minutes.

It wasn't just the inactivity and the isolation that were getting to her – it was the uncertainty. She had been found with the pills on her. If the analysis came back positive, how was she going to prove the Gems weren't hers? How could she hope to clear herself unless she got out there and did something positive?

Maddie made a decision. She stalked into her room and picked up her mobile. She scrolled through recent calls. Paul's number showed up. No such number. *Cute, Paul, really cute!*

She found Alex's number.

He picked up immediately. The sound of his voice was like a life line.

"Hi Maddie. Are you holding it together?"

"No, not really. Listen, I've had an idea. What if I call Laura and get her to ask Claire for a list of everyone who was at the party. I could make a few calls – find out if any of them know Paul or..."

"I don't think so, Maddie," Alex cut in. "Remember the conditions of your bail."

"I've got to do something, Alex," Maddie said. "I'm going crazy."

"Listen to me, Maddie." Alex's voice was calm but determined. "The bail conditions were that you can't go back to Cloud Nine and you can't make contact with any potential witnesses. You break either of those conditions and you're going to be in big trouble."

"I'm already in big trouble," Maddie said. "What could happen that would be worse?"

"You could get thrown out of PIC," Alex said sharply. "Police officers can't investigate themselves, Maddie. Think about that."

Maddie was silent. Frustrated anger was almost choking her.

"We're with you on this Maddie," Alex said. "But you have to trust us. Just keep your head down and I'll call you as soon as there's any news. OK?"

"Yes." Maddie ended the call and threw the mobile on her bed, a surge of anger erupting through her. She grabbed a chair and flung it across the room with all her strength.

It hit the wall with a splintering crash.

Maddie stood trembling, staring at the broken chair –

alarmed by the violence of her emotions. She turned on her heel and ran from the room, snatched up her house keys and slammed out of the flat.

She had to burn off some of that furious energy before she exploded.

❌

Muswell Hill, London, N10.

A phone call to the management of Cloud Nine had given Danny and Alex the address they needed. The top flat in a small mid-terrace house. The bell push had no name tag.

Alex rang. They waited.

Alex pressed again. The two other bells were labelled. R Thompson. M Lamble. He pressed those as well. If DJ Slikk wasn't in, then perhaps her neighbours might be able to help.

They heard the muffled thump of feet coming down the stairs.

"Result," said Alex.

The door opened.

A bleary-eyed woman with tousled blonde hair stared out at them. She was wrapped in a dressing gown.

"We're looking for DJ Slikk," Alex said.

"Sorry to disturb you," Danny added.

She opened the door a little wider, leaning on the

frame as she looked them up and down.

"Are you the Old Bill?" she asked.

"What makes you say that?" Danny asked.

She raised an eyebrow. "You don't look like door-to-door salesmen. And no one who cared about their personal safety would be dumb enough to ring my doorbell at this time of day unless they were here on official business. I work nights, you know? I need my beauty sleep."

"Are you DJ Slikk?" Alex asked.

"Only during working hours," she said. "Call me Sandy. I suppose you're here to ask me some questions about last night, yeah? About Paul?"

"What do you know about him?" Alex asked.

"Maybe we could do this inside?" Danny suggested.

She looked at him. "You can come into the hallway. But that's it."

She let them in. Danny closed the door. Sandy sat on the stairs, her dressing gown gathered around her. "Cloud Nine has a zero tolerance policy on drugs," she began. "Normally, if I'm suspicious of anyone, I give the stewards the whisper and they're chucked out pronto. But I wasn't sure about Paul – not to begin with."

"You were seen talking with him," said Alex. "Do you know him?"

Sandy shook her head. "He came over and started chatting – just hanging out. We talked about music and gigs and stuff. Then he said he knew a way to make the evening really fly. That made me suspicious. I pointed out Hackett to him. Hackett is our top bouncer – built like a brick wall. I said, 'See that guy over there? He can smell drugs from fifty metres. If he finds someone trying to deal drugs in here, he rips their legs off and stuffs them down their throat before he hands them over to the Old Bill. Get the picture?' Paul was super-cool. 'You think I'm a dealer?' he said. 'No way!'"

Sandy smiled a crooked smile. "So I said – what was all that about making the evening fly? He gave me a cute grin. 'I was talking about you and me getting together,' he said. 'I bet I know ways of lifting you off the ground.' So I pointed to Hackett again. 'He's my boyfriend,' I said. 'How about you go tell him what you just told me?'" Sandy laughed. "That was the last I saw of him – until a couple of hours later when that girl went down and Blondie did the first-aid business on her."

"Blondie?" Alex asked.

"The stunner that got arrested," Sandy said. "That was total nonsense, you know – that arrest. I was on my break – I was up there when the girl collapsed." Sandy's eyes were sharp. "I guess Paul managed to do some dealing after all, yeah? She took too much of something – that's my guess. But here's the killer – she was on the floor and Blondie was trying to help her – and I saw Paul go down beside her and put something into her bag. It was quick, and I wasn't sure, but I thought I saw a wad of notes – and maybe something else." She looked at Alex and Danny. "Drugs, I'm guessing. Then Paul got up and snaked off. I tried to follow him, but he did a really neat vanishing act on me. By the time I got back, Blondie had been arrested and it was all over."

"Why didn't you tell the police?" Danny asked.

She raised an eyebrow. "I thought I just had. Like I told you – the Old Bill marched in, scooped the girl up, and marched straight out again before I got back. I thought that was pretty strange. I've worked other places where there's been a raid. They usually lock the place down and ask a whole lot of questions before they let people go – but this time they seemed to know exactly who they were looking for."

"Would you be prepared to make a written statement of everything you've told us?" Danny asked.

"Sure. Blondie was set up, wasn't she? Who is she? Someone special?"

Alex smiled. "Thanks for your help, Sandy." He took out a notepad and scribbled the phone number for

Charing Cross CID. "These are the people who are dealing with the case. Call them and tell them everything you told us."

Sandy followed them to the door. "You're not the regular police, are you?" she said. "Who are you guys?"

Danny opened the door. "Just think of us as the men in black," he said.

"You're not wearing black," Sandy called after them as they walked down the path.

Danny turned at the gate. "We're in disguise," he said with a grin. "Do the right thing, Sandy – make that call."

They headed for the MSU.

Zoë had confirmed that Paul was dealing Gems – Sandy had said she'd seen him put something into Maddie's bag.

Two material witnesses. Things were beginning to look up for Maddie.

✺

London, W6.

568 Hammersmith Grove. Flat B.

The room needed decorating. The paintwork was yellowed with age, the wallpaper peeling from the walls. The cheap furniture was no better. There was an unmade bed.

A man sat at a table by the French windows. Through

the grimy glass, the garden could be seen – a mess of weeds and brambles.

The man was leaning close over a sheet of paper. Neatly ruled lines joined a series of names. It could have been a family tree – but it wasn't. It was a diagram of connections – person to person – leading up to a single name.

The man knew the diagram by heart, but he couldn't help returning to it, staring at it in cold anger.

One of several names at the foot of the page was circled.

Claire Petrie.

There was additional information: *18th Birthday Party – Cloud Nine*

A line led up to another name – *Laura Petrie.* A horizontal line was punctuated by several other names.

One of them was *Maddie Cooper* – also ringed.

A line led up from Maddie's name.

At the top of the page a final name had been scrawled in thick, hard capitals: *JACK COOPER.*

The man took a red pen and a ruler. He drew a very precise, neatly ruled gallows beside the name. He smiled. The pen came down again, drawing a stick man hanging from the red noose.

The door opened and a woman came into the room.

She picked up a jacket from the back of a chair and walked over to where the man was sitting.

"It's a quarter to two," she said. "I have to get back." She leant forwards and kissed the man's hair. "Ian? Are you listening? I have to get back to work."

He looked up at her and took her hand. "Listen, Red, why don't you take the afternoon off?"

She shook her head. "You know I can't do that." She slid her hand from his and picked up a black briefcase from the chair. "I have to play everything by the book. I'd be crazy to draw attention to myself now."

He frowned and nodded. "How are you handling things at work?" he asked.

"I'm handling it. Everything's fine." She stooped over the table, taking the pen from Ian's hand. "We're coming to get you, Chief Superintendent. Just you wait and see." She scribbled through Jack Cooper's name until it was obliterated.

Ian stood up and put his arms around her. "You and me, Red."

She kissed him. "Me and you," she said.

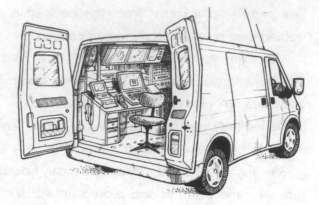

Chapter Six

Regent's Park.

Late afternoon.

Maddie was jogging hard and fast along Broad Walk. The zoo was behind her. She had just passed the wolf enclosure for the second time. She ran with grim, joyless persistence – circling the park with her head down and Xfm hammering into her head through her earphones.

She intended to plough on and on until she was too exhausted to run another step. Then she would take herself home – hopefully to collapse into sleep and get some relief from all this insanity.

The music from her radio was so loud that it was not until the news came on that she heard the chime of her mobile. She pulled her headphones off. The call was from Danny. She slowed but kept moving as she opened the line.

"Hey, Maddie – are you sitting down?"

"Not exactly," Maddie panted.

"We've got some hot news for you," Danny said.

Maddie listened as he told her of their investigations.

"Alex and I figure that once they get Sandy's statement, it's just a matter of time before you're back in."

It was as if a crushing weight had been lifted off Maddie's back. She let out a shout of joyful relief – leaping into the air and punching at the sky.

"Hey – careful with my eardrums!" Danny said, laughing.

"Sorry," Maddie gasped.

"We're heading to Control," Danny told her. "We're going to give the boss the good news."

A note of concern entered her voice. "Did Dad put you on this case? I thought he told me this morning that PIC were to back off."

"Uh... did he say that?" Danny stalled. "I guess we must have forgotten."

"You're going to be in so much trouble," Maddie said.

"No way," Danny said. "The boss is going to be so pleased with what we've discovered that we'll probably get promoted."

"Don't count on it," Maddie said. "But thanks – you don't know how much this means to me."

"You're embarrassing me, Maddie. Hey now – stay cool. We'll see you in the office, OK?"

"OK."

Danny cut the line.

Maddie lifted her head, her eyes shining, her face split by a wide smile.

She carried on jogging, but now the ground flew beneath her feet as she felt herself filled with a new energy and purpose.

✪

PIC Control.

DCS Cooper's office.

Danny and Alex stood side by side in front of Jack Cooper's desk. Alex had just given their report. Cooper had listened in stony silence, his face showing nothing.

It seemed to the two trainees that a very long time elapsed before their boss spoke.

"I told you categorically to keep out of this investigation," he said.

"Yes, boss," Alex said.

"You chose to ignore me."

"Yes, boss," Alex said.

Jack Cooper leant forwards, his eyes flickering from Danny to Alex. "If you ever disobey a direct order again, I'll cut you loose so fast that you'll get friction burns on the way out. Have I made myself clear?"

"Crystal, boss," said Danny.

There was another pause.

"I take it you've already spoken to Maddie," he said.

"Yes, boss. On the phone."

Jack Cooper nodded. "How did she react?"

"She screamed right in my ear, boss," Danny said. "I think she was pleased."

The very faintest flicker of a smile lifted the corner of Jack Cooper's mouth for an instant.

"We'll say no more about it, then," he said.

"Thank you, boss," said Alex.

"You're a star, boss," said Danny.

"Leave out the soft soap, Danny," said Cooper. "I take it that your unofficial jaunt around town has meant you've made no further progress on the meeting you're supposed to be setting up with that drug dealer you told me about?"

"It's top of the list, boss," Danny said. "I'm going to call my informant right now – the minute we get done here."

"See that you do. I want you to arrange a meet and I want an arrest report on my desk ASAP. Dismissed."

It wasn't until Alex and Danny had left his office that Jack Cooper allowed himself to smile. His daughter was off the hook. He reached for his phone.

"Get me DCS Reeves at Charing Cross please, Jackie," he said.

❂

The Coopers' flat.

A family meal.

20:35.

Maddie's life had taken a 180-degree turnabout in the past few hours.

Earlier that evening her father had called her to give her the official good news. He had spoken with the Chief Superintendent at Charing Cross. The two witness statements had tipped the balance in Maddie's favour – the investigation into the drugs found in her bag had moved on and she was in the clear.

The table was strewn with the debris of a large

Chinese takeaway. Gran had bought a bottle of Californian chardonnay to help celebrate the good news.

"To us!" she said, as their three glasses chimed together. She smiled at Maddie. "You can't keep a Cooper down!"

"You got that right!" Maddie laughed.

It was rare for the three of them to be together like this. Jack Cooper's job didn't often allow him the luxury of regular mealtimes. It made it all the more special for Maddie when circumstances allowed them to act like a normal family.

The Coopers had come through some seriously bad times together. On a terrible night only fifteen months ago, Maddie and her mother and father had been brutally shot down in the street. A gangland attack. Jack Cooper had been the prime target. He had survived, but he would spend the rest of his days in a wheelchair. Maddie's planned career as a dancer had been wrecked for ever by a bullet to the hip and – more terrible than anything Maddie could possibly have imagined – her mother had died in the attack.

Maddie's gran had helped them to pick up the pieces. It had taken a long time, but somehow, Maddie and her father had found the strength to carry on. Jack

Cooper had immersed himself in his work. Maddie had also discovered a new purpose – as a PIC trainee. It hadn't been until this had almost been snatched away that she had realised how important it was to her.

Maddie sipped the fragrant wine, looking at her father over the rim of her glass. "Are Danny and Alex in trouble?" she asked.

"Yes," he said.

She gave him an anxious look. "They only wanted to help me."

"I know," he said. There was a rare smile. "That's why I didn't skin them alive."

"What's going to happen next?" Maddie asked.

"Charing Cross will focus on trying to find Paul. He's the key. Get him and we get the lot of them. That's my belief." He looked at her. "They'll need you as a witness when they do pick him up."

Maddie's eyes gleamed. "I'm looking forward to it. It's a pity we're not involved in the case though. I'd like to get my hands on him. I'd show him what kind of an angel I am."

Her gran looked at her. "I beg your pardon?"

"Oh – it's nothing," Maddie said with a smile. "It's a personal thing between him and me." She looked at her father. "So, am I back on duty tomorrow?"

"You can be, if that's what you want," her father said. "But it might be a good idea for you to take a day off. Have a break – enjoy yourself."

Maddie thought for a moment. "I think I'll take you up on that." She gave her father a wide smile. "I could go shopping."

Her gran laughed. "You walked straight into that one, Jack. I think that's your cue to get your wallet out."

Chapter Seven

Wednesday morning.

10:47.

Maddie stepped out of the shower and went through to her room where the hi-fi system was pouring out some lazy RnB. She stood at the window and gazed out over the eccentric roofscape of London Zoo. The sky was clear and bright. The familiar sights of Regent's Park made her smile.

It was all so different from yesterday. The clouds were gone and her life was back on track. She had the day to herself and she was going to make the most of it. She hadn't finalised her plans, but she was considering several options. A trip to Covent Garden market would be cool – that, or a day of heavy-duty retail therapy in Oxford Street.

A pleasant thought struck her. Lunch with Alex and Danny maybe?

She turned the hi-fi down and stretched out on her bed. She reached for her mobile and switched it on. She'd give the guys a call – check out whether they were free to meet up with her sometime during the day.

There was a double beep.

A voicemail message.

She pressed Listen.

The voice was familiar. "Hello, Maddie. This is Paul. Remember? From Cloud Nine? I need to talk to you. Call me back as soon as you get this message. It's urgent."

She stared at her phone – taken completely by surprise. The last thing in the world she had expected was for Paul to make contact.

She hesitated for a moment, uncertain of how to deal with this. Alert Control? Call Alex or Danny? Speak with her father?

No. She was sick of being a victim. Paul had seen her as a soft target. She was going to prove him wrong. She was going to bite back. This time she would be ready

67

for him – smooth-talking Paul wasn't going to make a sucker out of her again.

She pressed Reply.

He picked up immediately.

"I got your message," she said, her voice calm but icy. "What do you want?"

"We need to meet," Paul said. "I want to help."

Maddie's eyes narrowed with suspicion. He sounded anxious – maybe even scared. Unless he was faking it.

"I'm listening," she said expressionlessly.

"I was paid to set you up. It was just a job – easy money. Five hundred to plant the tablets and the cash on you." There was a pause. "I like you. I don't want bad things to happen to you, OK?"

"What bad things?"

"Listen – the guy behind this is dangerous. He's got plans for you – I don't want you to get hurt. Meet me – I'll explain everything."

"Why are you doing this?" Maddie asked. "Conscience bothering you?"

"Something like that. I know this guy. You don't deserve to have him on your back. Meet me at three o'clock this afternoon at Earl's Court underground station. Call me on this number as soon as you get there – I'll tell you what to do."

"What's to stop me handing you over to the police?" Maddie asked.

"Do that and I say nothing. Earl's Court. Three o'clock. Don't tell anyone. Be on your own or I'm gone. Trust me, Maddie – you need to talk to me. That guy doesn't fool around." Something in Paul's voice sent a shiver down Maddie's spine. "The arrest was just a taster – he means to do you some serious harm. He's after your blood."

✪

PIC Control.

Danny sat on his desk, his feet up on the back of the chair. The telephone was on his knees. He was waiting for a call. Alex stood close by. One of Danny's informants was expected to make contact any time now.

"He's late," Alex said, glancing at his watch. Alex was not good at waiting around.

"It'll be cool," Danny said. He offered an open bag of M&Ms to Alex.

Alex shook his head.

The telephone rang. Danny counted to ten before picking up. "Good morning," he said, his voice suave and smooth. "You are through to Kid Gloves Executive Removals. My name is Daniel Dubbin, how may I help you?"

Alex smiled. Danny was great at that kind of thing.

"Ah, Mr Silver. Yes, I've been waiting for your call." Danny winked at Alex. "Yes, of course we can help you. Could you give me the details, please?"

In order safely to make contact with their networks of informants, PIC had set up a whole raft of bogus companies. Each had their own code words and their own telephone numbers. A call to Kid Gloves Executive Removals Ltd would come through to the PIC switchboard on a specific line. The Communications Officer in charge would then pass the call through to the appropriate agent. Anyone redialling or trying to trace the call would be routed through the same system. Everyone was covered. Everything was secure.

"You have an 1880 Eastlake Walnut Fainting Couch that you would like us to move for you," said Danny. "Certainly sir, I think we can help you with that. Where should we pick it up?" Danny scribbled the address. "Flat 401, Edinburgh Mansions, Moscow Road, Bayswater. Three fifteen this afternoon. Yes. I can't see any difficulties with that. Will you be there? No. Very well. That's not a problem. I'll be in contact regarding the fee once our business has been successfully concluded. Thank you for your custom. Please call again."

Danny put the phone down.

He smacked his hands together. The meet was on.

✪

Earl's Court station.

15:07.

The underground-train door slid open. Maddie stepped out on to the platform. The District Line. Westbound. This part of Earl's Court station was above ground level – partially canopied by a steel and glass roof.

There were very few people on the platform – this was the lull between lunch time and the late afternoon rush hour.

Maddie made her way towards the exits. She had two choices – up the stairs to the streets or down to the deeper tunnels of the Piccadilly Line. She paused, looking around. Where was Paul? She would have to call him.

In the few hours since she had spoken to him she had thought long and hard about what she was planning to do. Paul could have any number of reasons for luring her here. She could be walking into danger. Her father would have told her to back off. He would have handed the information over to Charing Cross CID. But if that happened, she wouldn't be allowed anywhere near Paul.

71

That wasn't good enough. She had a score to settle – he had put her through hell. She wanted to look into his eyes – to prove to him, and to herself, that she was able to deal with this.

She took out her mobile and flicked through to the number Paul had given her.

Paul answered in the middle of the first ringing tone.

"I'm here," she said. "Now what?"

✪

Paul Gilmore was sitting at the back of the last carriage of a train waiting at a District Line platform. There was only one other person in the carriage. A man – sitting with his back to Paul. Reading a newspaper.

Paul's clothes were drenched with nervous sweat. His hair was sticking to his forehead. His eyes flickered around. He had his mobile phone in his hand. He wiped his damp palms on his jeans.

Although he had been waiting for it, the sudden trill of his mobile phone startled him. He caught his breath – his heart hammering. He opened the line.

Maddie's voice: "I'm here. Now what?"

"Where are you?" Paul asked, keeping his voice low.

"District Line. Westbound platform."

"Good. Very good." There was relief in Paul's voice. "I'm in the train waiting at eastbound Platform 1. I'm in the last carriage. Make this quick, Maddie. It isn't safe for either of us."

He closed the line and slid the phone into his pocket.

His hands were shaking. Not long now. A matter of minutes.

He heard something behind him and turned his head. The man with the newspaper was standing right behind him.

The man shook his head. "Bad boy," he said.

❂

A narrow alley near the Hammersmith flyover.

Secluded. Deserted.

Harvey Silver turned into the alley – a small, dark-haired man in his early twenties. He walked along briskly, his shoulders hunched, his eyes wary.

Red stepped out of a deep-set doorway. Her arm snaked around Silver's neck. She pulled him back into cover. He coughed, clutching at her arm as she increased the pressure on his windpipe.

"Well?" she whispered, her scarlet mouth close to his ear.

"You're choking me," he gasped.

She relaxed her grip. Silver stared at her with wide, frightened eyes.

"I made the call," he said. "He went for it – sweet as a nut. Didn't suspect a thing. He'll be there at three fifteen." He blinked up at the woman. "I did what I was told – there's no need for strong-arm stuff."

She smiled and released him. He tottered back and hit up against the side of the doorway. He eyed her uneasily.

"Where's my money? I was promised 100 pounds."

Red drew a wedge of bank notes out of a pocket. She casually peeled off five twenty-pound notes and let them flutter to the ground.

Silver knelt to retrieve them.

Red walked quickly away, the click of her heels echoing loudly as she strode along the silent alley.

Harvey Silver's eyes followed her. "Nice doing business with you," he murmured. He crammed the money into a pocket and slithered off in the opposite direction.

Ten seconds later, the alley was empty again.

✪

Maddie was on Platform 1. She walked the length of the standing train. There were only a handful of people on board.

She came to the last carriage and stepped inside.

The carriage was empty except for one figure –

sitting with his back to her – way down at the far end.

Paul.

She made her way through the carriage.

He didn't move.

She could feel the blood pulsing through her temples. The quietness was unnerving in such a public place. Almost unnatural. Threatening.

She came to the seated figure. His head was forward – as though he was reading something in his lap. Reaching out, she gingerly touched his shoulder. Her dry mouth made it impossible to speak. Her heart was hammering and her hand shook.

She pushed at his shoulder.

As if in slow motion, he folded in on himself and slumped, loose-limbed, to the floor of the carriage.

Then she noticed the blood.

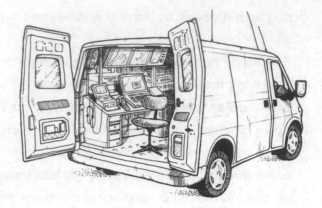

Chapter Eight

Maddie stared down at the twisted, crumpled shape on the floor of the underground train. The shock punched up into her throat, wanting to release itself in a cry. She stifled it, ignoring the quaking of her limbs, the sickness welling up from deep in her stomach.

She knew that he was dead even before she crouched to confirm it.

She pressed her fingers inside his collar, feeling for the carotid pulse. She looked all around her – staring down the empty length of the carriage – scanning the platform through the graffiti-spattered windows.

There was no pulse. Blood was creeping out from under the body.

The horrified sixteen-year-old girl in Maddie wanted to run away, but the PIC trainee knew that wasn't an option. Dreadful as it was, she had work to do – and fast.

She stood up and moved swiftly to the open door. She placed her shoulder bag in the doorway. It would block the door if it tried to close and save her from being trapped on this train with Paul's dead body – and maybe even with his murderer.

She went back to the body. Crouching down, she took a long deep breath, mentally preparing herself for the ordeal.

She turned him over. His chest was a mass of blood. It must have been a knife – or a silenced gun.

She had to put her feelings on hold – there would be plenty of time for her to give in to revulsion and fear later. "Don't think about it, Maddie – just do your job," she whispered softly to herself.

Easier said than done.

Her training came back to her. She ran her fingers expertly over him – testing his lapels and cuffs and seams for signs of anything hidden. She checked his shoes and his socks, and ran her fingers inside the waist of his jeans – checking for a body-belt. She felt inside the bloodied collar of his shirt for anything hanging around his neck.

That was the taught order of rapid searching: secret hiding places first, obvious places last.

She went through his pockets. There was a leather wallet. A black plastic cardholder, a bunch of keys, a Swiss Army Knife and some loose change. Half a pack of spearmint gum. An underground train ticket. Sunglasses in a soft sheath. A slimline mobile phone.

Maddie stiffened as a loud metallic hissing sounded in the carriage. The train rattled and hummed as the engines were readied for departure.

She gathered Paul's things and went back to the door. She picked up her bag, tipping the items inside, hitched it on to her shoulder and stepped off the train just as the doors slid shut behind her.

Glancing around, she forced herself to remain calm. The train began to move. Unsettling as the silence had been, the noise of the accelerating train was much more frightening. Cloaked by the noise, a murderer could creep dangerously close.

Maddie began to walk rapidly towards the exit. Her brain was speeding – Paul had been killed in the time it had taken her to get here from the westbound platform. A couple of minutes – that was all.

He had said there was a man who wished her harm. Somehow, the man must have suspected that Paul was going to betray him – meaning he must have known Paul was going to meet her here. He could still be close by – watching her – waiting to strike.

Maddie speeded up, trying not to panic. But the rush and clamour of the departing train was too much for her. She saw stairs leading down and made a darting movement towards them. She took the steps three at a time, one hand clinging to the metal rail. She almost fell.

She raced along a tiled hallway. There were a few people down there. A couple of them glanced at her as she ran. There was nothing unusual about a young woman running along a corridor at Earl's Court station – she could be late for an appointment – running to catch a train – running to meet her boyfriend. Running for her life.

In front of her were escalators leading down to the Piccadilly Line.

Paul's murderer could be standing in a quiet corner – a gun trained on her – his finger tightening on the trigger.

Maddie bounded down the metal steps and ran

along another corridor. It divided abruptly. She could go either to the left or the right – eastbound or westbound platform. If there had been a train waiting, it would have made her choice – she would have leapt aboard to be sped away from this terrible place. But there were no trains waiting. Just a scattering of mid-afternoon travellers – any one of whom could be the murderer.

She saw a flight of spiral stairs leading up. A sign: *THIS STAIRWAY HAS 83 STEPS – USE ONLY IN AN EMERGENCY.*

She heard someone shout. She ignored it.

Maddie pounded up the steps, keeping tight to the hub of the spiral. Her foot slipped on the narrow tread and she stumbled, cracking her shin against the brutal metal edge. Biting back a cry of pain, she found her footing and carried on climbing.

She heard the thudding of footsteps following her. She didn't pause to look back. Gasping for breath, she came to the head of the stairs. There was a doorway which led back to the eastbound District Line platform. She had virtually run in a circle.

Maddie pressed herself against the wall. She could hear the hammering of her pursuer's feet. He was getting closer. She tensed her muscles.

A man emerged from the doorway.

She sprang at him.

He raised his arms to protect himself as she struck out.

He took a step backwards – his foot hanging for a moment in the air as he teetered at the head of the stairs. He grabbed at her to save himself, but she was still moving forwards.

Maddie felt her balance tip. She stared down the dark metal gulf of the stairway as he dragged her over the edge.

❂

Edinburgh Mansions, Bayswater.

15:13.

It wasn't the classiest place in London. Danny had pointed that out to Alex as they had stepped into the old-fashioned lift. It clanked and shuddered as it took them to the fourth floor.

They had worked together on meets like this before – they had a formula. Danny did the talking and Alex stood in the background, looking menacing. As Danny often said, Alex did menacing like a pro.

The lift doors clattered open. They came out into a narrow corridor. Deep red flock wallpaper absorbed the yellowish light from the wall fittings.

Danny was carrying a small holdall. It contained £10,000 in cash – requisitioned from PIC funds. He checked door numbers. He gestured for Alex to follow.

Danny looked at his watch. It was three fifteen exactly. "I like to be punctual," he said. "It's only polite."

"What's the secret signal for today?" Alex asked.

Danny thought for a moment. If either of them suspected there was going to be trouble, it was important for them to warn one another. They had backup – four armed agents in a car close at hand, waiting for the word from Alex's throat mike. But things could turn ugly in a matter of seconds. Undercover police officers had been found dead in nicer places.

"If either of us say, 'do you guys like M&Ms?' – it's a bust and we get out pronto," Danny said.

They found flat 401.

They looked at one another.

Danny knocked.

The door opened within four heartbeats.

The man was wearing an open-necked Ben Sherman shirt and jeans.

A second man was sitting on a narrow bed. He was the older of the two – late thirties, Danny judged. The boss of the outfit. There was a closed briefcase at his side.

He stood up as they entered and shook hands with Danny. "Mr Dubbin?" he asked.

"Call me Danny." He smiled. "Mr Silver recommended you to us. I wasn't given a name."

"Phil," said the first man. "This is Trevor – he'll want to give you and your colleague a quick pat-down, if that's OK."

"Sure," Danny said. "You can't be too careful. But we're not carrying."

Trevor frisked Danny and Alex for weapons. He missed the tiny throat mike in Alex's lapel.

Alex made eye contact with Trevor. He was obviously muscle. If things went wrong, Trevor would need to be taken out quickly. Alex appraised him. The face was hard and there was an unusual intelligence in the eyes. Trevor would need watching.

"They're clean," Trevor said.

"Then we can do business," said Phil.

Alex positioned himself by the door.

Trevor stood close by, not looking at him, but obviously poised to react if Alex made any sudden moves.

Danny perched on the arm of a padded chair. Phil sat down on the bed again. He lifted the briefcase up.

Danny placed his holdall on his knees – aiming the

hidden CCD video camera towards Phil. "So what have you got for us?" he asked.

"What are you in the market for?" Phil asked. "We can provide you with horse – snow – crack – blow – speed. Best quality – in any quantities you can move." He smiled. "Name your flavour, Danny."

"We're looking to score some Gems," Danny said. "I was told you were the main supplier around here."

"How much do you want to spend?"

Danny patted the holdall. "I've got ten grand here – will that do you for a start?" he smiled. "If the quality is up to standard, we'll be needing a constant supply."

"Not a problem," Phil said. "I haven't heard the word on you, Danny – are you new in town or what? Fresh over from the States and looking for some action?"

Alex's eyes narrowed. There was something wrong here. The man was stalling. Why? Phil's hand was on the briefcase. The movement was subtle, but Alex noticed it. He had slightly changed the angle of the case – a move a person might make if they had a hidden camera and wanted to make sure the subject was centre frame.

Alex took a step forwards. Trevor moved to intercept him.

"Do you guys like M&Ms?" Alex said.

Danny looked sharply around at him. He half-rose.

"Take them!" Phil shouted.

Alex aimed a blow at Trevor's head. It was deflected with deceptive ease. Alex made the follow-through but Trevor sidestepped and brought clasped hands down hard on the back of Alex's neck. He crashed to the ground. Trevor came down on top of him – knees tight into his back, his hands dragging Alex's arms back – locking him in position.

"Sit down, Mr Dubbin." Danny found himself staring into the business end of a gun.

He sat.

"Do we have a problem here, Phil?" he asked.

Chapter Nine

Maddie threw her arm out as she fell forwards into the well of the spiral staircase. Her fingers managed to snatch hold of the metal banister rail. The man was still clutching at her, his eyes full of fear. Her arm was almost pulled from its socket as their combined weight threatened to wrench her fingers loose.

But she held on. The two of them swung heavily against the central pillar of the spiral. She scrabbled to regain her footing. The man was sprawled on the stairs.

She hooked her hand into his collar and pulled him to his feet.

"Let go of me," he panted, his eyes wide as he stared at her. "Are you mad?"

"Who are you?" Maddie demanded.

"I work here," said the man.

She frowned, suddenly unsure. "Why were you following me?"

"You looked like you were in trouble," he gasped. "I thought you might need some assistance."

She stared at him. He was wearing a blue shirt and charcoal grey trousers. "You work in the station?"

"Yes. In the office." He indicated a photocard attached to his shirt pocket. The man was beginning to pull himself together after the shock of Maddie's attack. "I saw you running. I thought maybe someone had frightened you. I only wanted to help."

Maddie released her grip. The man stared warily at her.

"I'm sorry," she breathed. "Did I hurt you?"

"Just my pride," he said. He straightened his collar. "You're not the kind of girl who needs a knight in shining armour, are you?"

Maddie threw him an apologetic half-smile. "Not often," she said. "But thanks for the thought. Are you sure you're all right?"

"I'm fine," he said.

"What's the quickest way out of here?" she asked.

"The Warwick Road exit," he replied. He pointed upwards. "Take those stairs – then follow the walkway."

"Thanks."

"My name's Gary," he called after her. "My shift finishes at five o'clock, if you'd like to..."

But she was already out of earshot – running up the stairs towards the walkway.

✪

Edinburgh Mansions.

Flat 401.

Alex was sitting with his back to the wall. He had underestimated Trevor. The man had taken him down quickly and efficiently, and he now found himself staring up at a gun.

Danny was sitting on the bed, his hands raised at shoulder level.

"We seem to have offended you somehow, Phil," he said. "What can I say to put things right between us?"

"Shut it," came the reply.

"What's with the pro-wrestling treatment?" Danny asked. "I thought we were here to do business."

Phil slipped his hand into his pocket. He pulled out a wallet. He flipped it open and held it up in front of Danny's face.

Danny focused on what he was being shown. His heart sank.

"Oh – great!" He groaned. He looked around at Alex. "You're not going to believe this..."

It came without any warning.

The door burst open. A man crouched in the doorway, his arms stretched forwards, both hands clasping a gun.

"Drop your weapons or I will open fire!" he shouted.

Two more men stood directly behind him – also aiming weapons into the room.

Trevor's gun turned to the doorway. "We're police officers!" he yelled. "Put your gun up."

The man edged into the room – moving the aim of his gun from Phil to Trevor, his eyes narrow and watchful.

Danny's voice broke into the tense silence. "Let's not get all Hollywood here, guys," he said. He looked at Phil. "May I reach for my ID card?"

Phil nodded. "Slowly."

Danny drew out his PIC pass and showed it to the man.

Anger flooded Phil's face. "What the..."

Danny looked around at his back-up team. "They're Special Branch," he said.

The guns were lowered. Trevor helped Alex to his feet.

"This meeting was supposed to be the payoff for three months' work in deep cover," Phil said. He glared at Danny. "Do you want to tell me what the hell PIC think they're doing, sending you idiots in to foul everything up?"

Danny tipped his head back. He closed his eyes and let out a long breath.

"We've been suckered," he said. "Next time I see Harvey Silver, I'm going to teach him a lesson that he'll never forget!"

✪

Maddie was still shaking from her encounter with the unfortunate young London Underground employee. That had been stupid – she had panicked. She needed to get a grip. But she also needed to get out of there.

She ran along the raised walkway. She turned left and then right. There were the barriers, and beyond them the open street. There seemed to be an unusual number of people milling about out there.

She passed through the barrier and came out into bright sunshine. The Earl's Court Exhibition Centre stood back from high railings on the far side of the street. Crowds of people were coming and going.

Maddie saw a banner: *MURDER! THEFT! SUSPENSE! The Mystery Club Convention.*

She glanced over her shoulder. There was no sign that anyone was following her, but she still felt unsafe.

She stepped forward into the crowd. If Paul's murderer was on her trail, it would be easier for her to lose him in amongst all these people.

She moved through the crowd, constantly watchful – crossing the road – getting away from the station entrance. But what she really needed was somewhere secluded where she could lie low for a little while to catch her breath.

A thought struck her. She knew a quiet place – not far from here. She pushed against the tide of people making their way into the Exhibition Centre. Eventually she managed to break free and began to run along Warwick Road. As she turned right into Old Brompton Road, she was confronted by the high black railings and tall stone entrance to Brompton Road Cemetery. She ran across the road, glancing back – still unsure of her safety.

She broke into a sprint – running in under the high arch. The old cemetery opened out on front of her. She ran along the central path. All round were lichen-stained gravestones and age-worn mausoleums, guarded by crumbling angels and overgrown by tall grasses and dark, creeping plants.

One particular stone structure caught her eye. The family tomb of Benjamin Golding MD. An ivy-strangled tree stood to one side, affording deep shade. She took one final look over her shoulder, then sprang sideways and pushed her way into the gloom.

Maddie sat cross-legged on a blanket of ivy, pausing to catch her breath and to gather her wits. The image of Paul's dead body drifted into her head. She forced the dreadful vision away, refusing to succumb to the horror of it.

She pulled her shoulder bag around into her lap and drew out Paul's belongings.

Activating his phone, she opened the menu and scrolled through a long list of names and addresses.

Useful stuff.

She went through his wallet. There was a picture of a dark-haired girl. Maddie wondered whether it was Paul's girlfriend. She swallowed hard at the thought of the terrible news that smiling girl would soon be receiving.

Maddie put the wallet to one side and picked up the credit-card folder. It felt slippery. She looked at her fingers. They were wet with blood.

She shuddered and dropped the folder.

She brought her knees up to her chest, hiding her face in her arms as the full shock of what she had seen finally hit her.

It was some time before she felt able to take out her own mobile and make the call to Control.

○

568 Hammersmith Grove. Flat B.

A long time ago, someone had painted the bathroom walls with two clashing tones of pink. The tiles over the sink were grey and cracked. Limescale stained the taps and left a brown residue around the plughole.

Ian was leaning forwards, washing his hands in front of the mottled mirror. His face was still, his jaw muscles clenched, his eyes dead and cold. Then he smiled and winked at his reflection. Whistling between his teeth, he picked up the soap again and continued to wash.

Red came into the bathroom, stood behind him and slid her arms around his waist. She noticed the gun that lay by the basin.

"What happened?" she asked.

Ian smiled. "Paul was being naughty so I punished him. He won't be any more trouble. I could have got the girl, too, but I didn't want her to miss out on all the fun we've got planned." He stood up and began to towel his hands dry.

Red pressed her face against his and her eyes narrowed. "I've already skimmed enough money for the two of us to take a plane out of this country and never come back," she purred. "Why don't we do that? Why don't we just go?"

He turned and put his arms around her shoulders. His eyes burnt with an unblinking fever. "You know it's not just about that," he whispered. "I've got a score to settle before we leave. You don't want to spoil everything, do you?"

She shook her head. "Of course not. But I don't feel safe. We should do it soon, Ian. Get it over with."

"We will," he said. "And you're right – it's probably not safe for me to stay put for too long – not with Special Branch on my tail." His eyes glittered. "I know a place in Paddington. I can lie low there till I'm ready."

Red looked at him. "Will it be soon?" she asked.

"Oh yes," he said. "It'll be very soon."

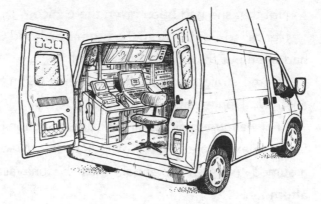

Chapter Ten

PIC Control.

16:12.

Maddie splashed water on her face. She looked at herself in the washroom mirror. The shock of the events at Earl's Court station seemed to be getting worse rather than better. She couldn't get the image of Paul's dead body out of her head. All she saw when she closed her eyes was the blood. And now she had to go into DCI Randal's office to talk the whole thing through for the record.

She didn't know if she could do that – not so soon after it had happened.

Not that she had been given the choice.

Her call to Control from the Brompton Road Cemetery had been put through to DCI Randal.

"Come straight in," he had told her. "Don't stop for anything. Don't wait. Get in here."

That was strange in itself – her direct Section Head was Susan Baxendale, not Kevin Randal. Maddie had assumed that DCI Baxendale must be unavailable that afternoon.

Maddie had arrived at Control to find that Jackie Saunders was missing from her desk. Her replacement told Maddie that Jackie had called in sick. Bad flu. Maddie couldn't remember the last time the Communications Officer had taken time off. She must have been feeling really bad.

She wasn't the only one.

Maddie gazed at her reflection. Pale face. Haunted eyes. No surprises there.

She pushed her hair back behind her ears, took a final look at herself in the mirror, then turned to head for the debrief with DCI Randal.

❏

"You did the right thing," Kevin Randal told her. "You kept your head and got yourself out of the firing line."

"I didn't keep my head," Maddie said. "I panicked. I

attacked an innocent man and nearly threw him down a flight of stairs."

Kevin Randal looked steadily at her. "You were neutralising what you saw as a potential threat. Was the man hurt?"

"No."

"Then you did exactly what you've been trained to do."

Paul's personal belongings were on the desk between them.

Maddie shivered. "I just left him there in the train," she whispered. She stared at Randal. "I shouldn't have done that – I shouldn't have left him there for someone else to find."

"The boy was dead – there was nothing you could have done for him," Randal said. "You were a potential target. Remember your basic training, Maddie. What's rule number one?"

Maddie swallowed hard. "To survive," she said.

"If it's a comfort to you, he was found by an officer of the London Transport Police," Randal told her. "The train was taken out of service. SO1's forensic team are on site. They'll call me if they come up with anything."

"Does my father know about this?" Maddie asked.

"Not yet. He was called away for a meeting with the

new Home Secretary. I'll file the report. He'll see it as soon as he gets back. He'll want to talk to you, I'm sure." He leant forwards, picking up Paul's phone. "So – what have we learnt so far?"

Maddie stared at him. How could he just move on to other business like that? Paul was dead. The boy's blood had been on Maddie's fingers. It wasn't something she could dismiss as if it was just another day-to-day incident.

Kevin Randal looked at her. "Problem?" he asked.

She didn't reply. What could she say?

He frowned, but there was sympathy in his face. "We can do this later if you need some time. But I have to warn you, Agent Cooper – it won't get any easier."

The use of her official title hit her like a splash of cold water. She wasn't just little Maddie who could crawl into a corner and hide. Not any more. She had responsibilities.

She lifted her chin. "I'm OK," she said determinedly. She focused on the mobile phone in DCI Randal's hand. "I've checked out the numbers Paul called recently," she said. She took out a notebook. "He made a lot of calls over the past few days to someone called Janey. She might be the girl in the photo in his wallet. He also called other people who are programmed into the phone." She consulted her notes. "Most of them seem to have nicknames or aliases. Scratchman – Sneaker – Dodgy –

Pit Bull. Until we start checking up on the numbers, we're not going to know whether they're just friends or whether they're drugs contacts."

"I'll get a team on to it," said Randal.

Maddie nodded. "We'll be able to feed his credit card details into The Frame and get his address." She looked at him. "I'd like to start processing the information straight away, if that's OK."

Kevin Randal nodded. "I'm sure you'll be able to find yourself somewhere to work," he said.

Maddie left the office, puzzling over that final remark. She would work at her usual desk, of course...

✪

But there was a stranger at Maddie's desk. A woman. She had black hair, a fine-featured pale face – very red lips and very dark eyes. She was dressed in a smart black suit. Maddie guessed she was probably in her mid-twenties.

"Hello," Maddie said.

The woman looked up from her work. She didn't speak.

"Excuse me," Maddie said. "This is my desk."

"I don't think so," said the woman, her voice clipped and icy. She turned back to her work as if Maddie was a fly she had just shooed away.

Maddie frowned. "Who are you?" she asked.

"Kathryn Grant," the woman said, not even looking up.

"I don't want to be rude," Maddie said, "but I need my desk back. I'm sure..."

The frozen voice cut her dead. "I'm busy," she said. "You'll just have to hot desk for the time being."

Maddie was completely taken aback by the woman's attitude. "What are you working on?" she asked.

Kathryn Grant didn't answer.

Maddie was starting to become annoyed. "I'm sorry?" she said, frostily. "I didn't hear what you said."

Kathryn stared up at her. "The more I'm interrupted, the longer I'll take."

"Hey Maddie! Great to see you!" Maddie looked around. It was Danny. "I see you've met Kat."

"Kathryn," she corrected him.

Danny looked at her with a faint smile. "Kat suits you better," he said.

Kathryn gave him a glacial look and then turned back to her work. Danny hooked his hand under Maddie's arm and led her over to the coffee machine.

"Who is she?" Maddie hissed. "What's she doing here?"

"Don't ask me," Danny said as he fixed Maddie a drink. "She's been here since first thing this morning –

and she's already got up everyone's noses. I call her Kat just to annoy her – Alex calls her the Ice Queen."

"I don't understand," Maddie said. "Is she a new Section Head or something? She acts like she owns the place. And why is she at my desk?"

"I can't tell you why she's here, but I can tell you who authorised her to use your desk."

"Good," Maddie said. "I'll have a few things to say to them, whoever they are."

Danny looked at her. "You'll have to wait till he comes back from his meeting with Maggie Churchill."

Maddie gaped at him. "My dad?"

Danny nodded.

Maddie stared over the open-plan office. She could see the back of Kathryn Grant's head over the low partition wall. Why had her father given her desk to another person – and exactly what was this arrogant woman's assignment?

●

Jack Cooper's office.

17:24.

For the second time in as many days, Alex and Danny were on the carpet in their boss's office. The first time had been their own fault – but this was different. Alex was angry. They had been set up by Danny's informant.

It had been a complete disaster.

"I've been running Harvey Silver for ten months, boss," Danny said. "He's always been right on the nail."

"Could he have been fed false information?" Jack Cooper asked.

"It's possible," Danny said. "But he's not some drug-soaked loser – he's sharp. He knows the score. And he's gone to ground. I haven't been able to make contact."

"Which suggests he knew you'd be looking for him," said Cooper.

"Just give us a day or two to find him," Alex said angrily. "I'll shake the truth out of him."

"I think we already know the truth, "Jack Cooper said. "He set you up so you'd walk right into a Special Branch sting."

"But why?" Alex said. "Was he hoping we'd lose it and start a gunfight in there? Did he want us to get killed?"

"No. I think the idea was to make us look like fools," Cooper said. "And he pulled it off nicely, didn't he? I've just spent fifteen minutes on the phone to the Head of Undercover Operations in Special Branch, trying to smooth things over. She's not happy. I don't blame her. We just compromised three months' work." He looked at Danny. "Silver is small fry, yes?"

Danny nodded.

"So it's not Silver we want," Cooper said thoughtfully. "We need the person who told him to set up the meet." He frowned. "There's a pattern here. Someone is trying to undermine us – to make us look like we can't keep our house in order. We need to know who is behind this. It isn't going to stop here. We need to get to them before they step up a gear and start to do some real damage."

There was a knock on the door.

"Yes?" Jack Cooper barked.

The door opened and Maddie stepped into the room. "Oh – sorry – I didn't realise you were with anyone," she said.

"Maddie. How are you feeling?" he asked. "That was a bad business at Earl's Court. We'll speak very soon, I promise."

"No, it's fine. I'm cool with it – really."

"I'll still need to talk to you about the report. But I'm afraid it'll have to wait a little while. Can you come back in thirty minutes?"

"Yes, but it wasn't that," Maddie said. "I'm trying to do some follow-up on Paul, but you put someone else at my desk. I keep getting moved around the office. It's really hard to work like that. Can't you put her somewhere else?"

Jack Cooper's response was swift and to the point.

"I'm sorry if you feel hard done by, Maddie, but I've got more important things to do than deal with that kind of trivia," he snapped. "Kathryn Grant stays where she is. You'll just have to make the best of it." He waved a dismissive hand. "I'll send for you later."

"Sorry." Maddie backed out of the room. She closed the door and stood staring at it for a few moments. She felt as if she'd been slapped.

"You OK?" Tara asked. Maddie looked around at her.

"He just more or less told me to run along and stop bothering him," Maddie said dazedly.

"You've caught him at a bad time," Tara said. "I was with him at the meeting with the new Home Secretary. She's started another round of cost cutting. She obviously wants to make a name for herself. PIC isn't a cheap department to run and your father thinks that she's going to come gunning for us."

Maddie looked at her. "You mean, she'll cut our funding?"

"I think your father's worried that she'll go the whole distance. She's a powerful woman, Maddie. Don't forget – Margaret Churchill has the authority to close PIC down for good."

Chapter Eleven

PIC Control.

18:10.

Maddie's working day was officially over but she had no intention of going home just yet. She had things to do. Alex offered to share his work station with her. She worked side-by-side with him, waiting for her father to call her into his office, but time passed and the call never came.

Maddie didn't mention Tara's fears about the Home Secretary. She didn't want to get the rumour-mill working. Morale was low enough after the drugs-bust fiasco — the last thing her colleagues needed was to hear that PIC was about to go down the tubes.

"This is just like when you started here," Alex reminded her as they worked. "Remember we were doing that trawl of incoming flights from America?"

Maddie nodded. She remembered it perfectly. It had led to her being kidnapped and almost killed. But it had also forged the strong bond between her, Alex and Danny.

She typed in her username.

The computer refused to acknowledge it.

She tried twice more with the same result.

"Someone else must already be logged in," Alex said.

Maddie frowned. "Kathryn Grant. Great. She's got my username as well as my desk." She looked at Alex. "Do you know what she's doing here?"

Alex shook his head. "I tried to check her out but it came up empty. She definitely doesn't work for a police department – or for the Home Office."

"She must be from somewhere important," Maddie mused. "Dad hates outsiders knowing our business."

"Maybe he wasn't given the choice," Alex said. He reached over and typed in his own username. The screen opened up.

Maddie accessed The Frame – the PIC database.

She picked her way through a series of case-specific

screens until she found what they needed.

She typed Paul Gilmore's credit-card number and clicked Search.

The Frame came up with the result in less than a second. Paul Gilmore lived in Mercers Road, Holloway, N19.

"I know that area," Maddie said. "It's just north of Camden Town." She clicked the mouse to exit.

The screen froze.

She tapped again. Nothing.

She slid the mouse across its pad, but the cursor didn't move.

She looked at Alex. "What's going on?" she asked.

"This might clear it." He pressed Alt, Control and Delete at the same time.

Nothing changed.

"Or it might not," Maddie said. "This is weird."

Alex frowned. He leant over and opened a drawer. Time to refer to the instruction manual.

"Alex – look!" Maddie's voice was urgent. Alex stared at the screen. A black ball had begun to bounce around the screen. In its wake, it left only blackness. The ball careered from side to side – from top to bottom of the screen, faster and faster, spreading a thickening web of nothing.

Maddie heard shouts from around the room.

"It's a virus," Alex said.

A few seconds later the bouncing ball had done its work – Maddie was staring at a completely blank screen.

Alarmed voices rose around her – it sounded as if every computer on the floor had been hit.

The PIC computers were heavily firewalled – it should have been impossible for this to have happened.

The same questions occupied everyone at Control as they tried to get a grip on the situation. How had a virus got into their system – and what damage had it done?

Every computer in the entire PIC network had been affected. The virus had hit without warning, provoking a mainframe crash of unprecedented proportions.

Maddie noticed Kathryn Grant in angry conversation with Tara.

"I need to see DCS Cooper immediately," Grant was saying.

"Not possible, I'm afraid," Tara said.

"You don't seem to understand," Kathryn Grant said. "I believe this may have been done deliberately to sabotage my work."

"What work might that be, Miss Grant?" Tara asked.

Kathryn Grant glared at her. "Do I get to see DCS Cooper or not?"

Tara shook her head.

"Then it's pointless for me to remain here," Kathryn Grant said. "Tell DCS Cooper that I am reporting this to my superiors." She gave Tara a final haughty look. "Have the courtesy to let me know when you're back on line."

"I'll be sure to make that my absolute priority," Tara said icily.

Kathryn Grant stalked away. Two minutes later she was gone from the office.

Tara smiled at Maddie. "She's a charmer, isn't she?" she said.

"Tell me about it," said Maddie. She looked at Tara. "Why would she think the virus was aimed at her?"

"I have no idea," said Tara.

"Do you know what she's doing here?"

"I'm afraid not," said Tara. "I wish I did."

Time went by. Maddie watched helplessly as she saw Section Heads and IT support staff try and fail to put things right. As the minutes ticked by, Maddie gradually began to realise just how disastrous this could be. PIC was hugely dependent on its computers – all files, folders, case histories, archives and active operations were now locked down in the frozen system. There was virtually nothing on paper. If the virus had irretrievably crashed the mainframe, years of work could have been lost.

Emergency meetings took place as Section Heads tried to pull something together. PIC couldn't simply shut down – its agents couldn't just sit there playing wastepaper basketball until things got fixed.

As the evening deepened into night, the news got steadily worse.

Kevin Randal came from a brief meeting with Jack Cooper, his face drawn with new concern.

He gathered people around him. "It's worse than we thought," he said. "The virus hasn't just affected us – it's ripped right through Cobra. Everything is down."

Cobra – the UK's Internal Defence Programme. That meant that every Home Office Security Unit was out of commission. This went way beyond crime fighting – if Cobra wasn't up and running again soon, the country's entire security system would be blind.

Worse was still to come.

"It's beginning to look as though the virus was introduced internally," Kevin Randal told them.

"From within Cobra?" Alex asked.

Kevin Randal looked at him. "From within PIC," he said.

Maddie stared at him. "That's not possible. Unless someone did it without realising."

"Let's hope that's the case." Kevin Randal looked around at the concerned faces. "I'll need to speak with everyone who has plugged an external CD or floppy disk into the system over the past five days – and I'll want to know every Internet site you people have visited over the same period. That virus got in here somehow – I intend to find out how."

Maddie looked at Alex. "Could someone have done it deliberately?" she asked.

"We'll address that question if it becomes necessary," Randal said. "In the meantime, we'll assume it was introduced unwittingly. I don't need to tell you that the Home Secretary has gone ballistic. She's sending in a crack IT team from GCHQ."

"Are we getting the blame for this?" asked Alex.

Kevin Randal looked grimly at him. "Margaret Churchill's exact words were: 'Do nothing. I'm going to send in a team that I can trust to clear up yet another of your messes.'" He looked around. "Tell me – do those sound like the words of a happy Home Secretary to you?"

Maddie stared uneasily at him. This disaster might be the final straw that would convince the Home Secretary to pull the plug on PIC.

"In the meantime," Kevin Randal said, "we have to keep things going as best we can till the IT team arrives. We can still use the telephones, the fax machines and the laptops. PIC agents are known for being able to think on their feet – here's your chance to prove it." He strode away. "And will someone try to find out where DCI Baxendale has got to?" he shouted. "She needs to be here!"

Jack Cooper hadn't emerged from his office since the virus had struck. Maddie could only imagine what he was going through in there – making desperate phone calls to his influential contacts – trying to keep a lid on the turmoil – trying to hold things together.

Trying to save PIC.

✪

The Coopers' flat.

22:07.

Maddie had been home for fifteen minutes – just long enough for her to take a shower while her gran made a late supper for the two of them.

Maddie sat at the table in her robe, her wet hair wrapped in a towel, quietly talking her gran through the afternoon from hell.

"I'd only been talking to Paul on the phone a couple of minutes before I found him. And then..." She swallowed. "It was awful, Gran."

Her gran rested her hand on Maddie's arm. "The important thing is that you're all right," she said.

Maddie smiled weakly. "That's what DCI Randal said. Rule one: survive."

"I like that rule," her gran said.

Maddie stood up and crossed to the sink where she poured a glass of water.

"Just before I left work, I asked Tara when she'd be bringing Dad home," she said, taking a swig of water. "She doesn't think he'll be prepared to leave Control. I haven't even seen him since the virus hit."

"It was the last thing he needed right now," her gran said. "He's been under constant stress since Margaret Churchill became Home Secretary. There's no love lost there. I just hope he doesn't overdo it – you know what he's like. He'll work himself into the ground."

"Tara's with him," said Maddie, putting the glass down and leaning on the kitchen counter. "She'll make sure he eats and gets some rest."

"Well, I hope so. He's as stubborn as..." Her gran smiled. "As you are."

Maddie sighed, smiling lightly. "I think the Home Secretary is blaming Dad for the computer crash. It looks like the virus was introduced at Control – although no one has figured out how yet."

"Those things are very sophisticated these days," said her gran. "It'll probably be something as simple as an infected email."

"I hope so," Maddie said thoughtfully. "Because if it isn't something like that, then we've got real problems."

Her gran looked enquiringly at her.

"If it wasn't introduced by accident, then someone working at PIC must have done it deliberately," Maddie said. "And if that's the case – who can we trust any more?"

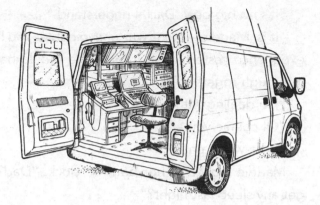

Chapter Twelve

The Coopers' flat.

Maddie's bedroom.

06:45.

Maddie was woken by the ringing of her mobile. She snatched it off the bedside cabinet.

"Maddie. It's me."

She sat up, forcing herself to concentrate. "Dad?"

"Were you asleep?" Jack Cooper asked.

"Yes, but it's OK." She rubbed her hand over her eyes. "Do you need me at Control?"

"No. I wanted to apologise to you, Maddie. I should have made time to see you yesterday. I let you down."

"It's no big deal, Dad. I understand."

"It is, Maddie – but it was unavoidable. You had a bad experience yesterday afternoon. We should have talked it through together."

"I'm dealing with it, Dad."

"Of course you are."

There was a pause.

Maddie looked at her bedside clock. "Dad? Did you get any sleep last night?"

He paused. "Yes."

"You are such a bad liar."

"Listen, Maddie – as soon as this crisis is over, we'll have a long talk. That's a promise."

"Don't worry about me, Dad. I'm a big girl now."

A tone of mock authority came into his voice. "I think you can let me decide when to stop worrying about you, Madeleine."

She laughed softly. "Yes, boss," she said.

"I have to go now. I need to make yet another bridge-building call to the Home Office."

"Poor you. Is it bad?"

"It's been better."

"OK. I'll see you later. And eat something, Dad. That's an order."

Her father laughed quietly. "Yes, boss," he said.

PIC Control.

07:48.

The lift doors opened and Maddie stepped into a world of chaos. The clatter of keyboards and the hum of printers and servers had been replaced by the sound of running feet and of voices calling out information across the office.

Alex was at the Communications Desk.

He looked up at Maddie. "Welcome to the new stone age," he said. "One direct hit and the whole system has collapsed. We'll be sending out smoke signals next."

"Is everything still down?" she asked.

"Down and out," said Alex. The switchboard lit and he took a call. He patched it through.

"Is Jackie still off sick?" Maddie asked.

Alex nodded. "We're taking it in turns to cover for her." He looked around. Agent Cassandra Shaw was approaching.

"My turn in the hot seat," she said. Alex took off the headset and vacated the desk. He and Maddie walked through the office. Tables had been pushed together and referencing maps spread out across them. Agents were at their desks, writing notes for the fax machines by

Others were speaking into mobile phones, maintaining contacts that would usually have been dealt with in seconds through the Internet.

"How long have you been on shift?" Maddie asked.

"Only for a couple of hours," Alex said.

Maddie looked at him. "Since half past five?"

Alex smiled. "We still have the same amount of work to do – the bad guys haven't slowed down."

"I should have been here," Maddie said.

"The boss thought you needed a break. You had a bad day yesterday." He looked carefully at her. "I'm not going to ask you how you feel. It takes a long time to come to terms with something like that – and you never get used to it."

"Did my dad get any sleep do you know?" she asked.

"I don't think so," Alex said. "He's taking all this very personally."

Maddie looked at him. "Do you think it could have been an inside job?" she asked, her voice low, as if she was speaking treason.

"Not a chance," Alex said. "The GCHQ team will find out how our firewall was breached. Then they'll reinforce it to make sure it never happens again."

"Is anyone on follow-up with the stuff I got from Paul?"

"Kevin put a couple of guys on the phones and there are another three out in the field, foot-slogging to the addresses we've managed to track down." He shook his head. "Nothing positive so far. Danny's still out hunting for Harvey Silver."

Kevin Randal came over. "I need someone to check out Paul Gilmore's home address," he said.

"I'll do it," Maddie said.

"OK. But not on your own."

A new voice sounded. "I'll go with her." It was Tara. She looked tired. "The boss just kicked me out," she explained. She looked at Maddie. "He said I was nagging him worse than you. He's up there living on nerve ends and black coffee. If he doesn't take a proper break soon, the computer won't be the only thing to crash."

Maddie looked at Kevin Randal. "Put a call through to my gran," she said. "She knows how to deal with him."

"I'm on it," said Kevin. He looked at Tara and Maddie. "You be careful out there. Someone is targeting us – don't get taken by surprise."

☾

Mercers Road, Holloway, N7.

Maddie and Tara used Paul's own keys to get access to his flat. It was in a house conversion. First floor.

119

The kitchen and bathroom were at the back of the house – living room and bedroom to the front. Tara headed for the kitchen.

Maddie went into the bedroom. She stood by the unmade bed, gazing around at Paul's things. Clothes that he hadn't got around to putting away. An open book face-down on the bedside cabinet. A jacket hanging off the edge of the door. A mug with a scum of stale coffee in the bottom.

Maddie felt a sense of desolation. He would never come back to put those clothes away, to wash up the dirty mug, to finish the book. She pressed the heels of her hands into her eyes – seeing again his body crumpled on the tube-train floor. Seeing the seeping blood.

She raked her fingers back through her hair. "No," she told herself firmly. "I don't have time for this." She had a duty to Paul – and a duty to PIC to find out who had killed him.

She fingered through some papers and letters on the sideboard. Junk mail, mostly – a couple of bills. Nothing relevant. She emptied his drawers, working methodically – laying the contents carefully on the floor, pulling the draws out, upending them to check for anything taped to the undersides or the backs. There was nothing.

She went through his wardrobe. From the kitchen, she could hear the sounds of Tara searching. Tara's presence comforted her. She was a good person to have at your side if things got out of hand. Tara was a martial arts expert. A black belt.

Maddie turned to the bed. She stripped the duvet off, feeling it for secret pockets. She lifted the mattress. A corner of brown leather was revealed. She pulled it out.

A Filofax. She dropped the mattress back into place. She knelt on the floor, popped the clasp and opened the Filofax. There was a page of personal details.

The flat had become absolutely quiet.

She turned a page. There were addresses.

One caught her eye.

PIT BULL – Flat B, 568 Hammersmith Grove.

She recognised the name from the address book in Paul's mobile phone, but she had no time to search further. A heavy impact on the back of her head drove her to the floor. There was a blinding moment of pain and nausea – and then she was swallowed by absolute darkness.

Chapter Thirteen

PIC Control.

The canteen.

10:40.

Danny had just come in from a frustrating morning on the streets. He and Alex were taking a quick break – coffee and sandwiches snatched between shifts. Not that the idea of shifts meant much right then – people worked the hours needed to get things done. Not many agents were allowing themselves the luxury of going home. The top-floor recreation suites had provision for brief catnaps as and when possible.

Down on the other three floors of PIC Control, the

GCHQ IT team were hard at work. They had two goals: to get PIC up and running again as quickly as possible and to find out how the bouncing-bomb virus had got in there.

Danny had problems of his own.

"Silver has vanished off the face of the earth," he told Alex. "I've been all over. I've spoken to all his homeboys. He hasn't been seen for two days."

"Someone paid him to set us up and now he's off spending the money," Alex said.

"He's got to surface sometime," Danny growled. "And I'll be waiting for him when he does." He looked at Alex. "One of our meeting places was Pret A Manger in Soho – I went there to have a chat with some people." He raised an eyebrow. "And I was told something very interesting. You remember Sammi?"

Alex nodded. Sammi worked at Pret – she was friendly with most of the PIC agents.

Danny leant across the table and lowered his voice. "Guess who she saw having a cosy lunch in a dark corner of the café yesterday? Susie B – and a guy who, judging by the description she gave me, was Andy Blake."

Alex frowned. "The head of Special Branch recruitment?" he said. "What would Susan Baxendale want with him?"

Danny shrugged. "My thoughts exactly. Why is one of our Section Heads talking to a guy whose job is head-hunting top people from other departments?"

Alex frowned. "You think she's about to jump ship?"

"Susie B is nobody's fool," said Danny. "Perhaps she knows something we don't."

"Like what?"

"Like we're in even bigger trouble than we think," said Danny. "Like PIC is about to hit an iceberg..."

✪

The first thing that Maddie was aware of was a thunderous pain in her head. She opened her eyes. The light pierced in. She could feel someone turning her. She could hear a voice but she couldn't make out the words. The world was an agonising blur.

She was lying on the floor. The pain in her head was so intense that even the slightest movement made her gasp.

"Come on, Maddie." She squinted up into a familiar face. "Are you OK?" It was Tara.

Maddie groaned. "Feel... sick..."

"Let me help you up."

Maddie struggled to her feet, blinded by the pain. She was led to the bathroom, where she fell on to her knees over the toilet. She retched.

She felt something cool on her face. Tara was

patting her skin with a wet towel.

"Did you see her?" Tara asked.

Maddie struggled to form words. "See... who...?"

"The woman who hit you."

Maddie shook her head. The pain blazed. She focused on Tara's face. Tara had a raw graze across her left cheek. Blood was trickling down into her collar.

"What happened?" Maddie asked.

"We were bushwhacked," Tara said. "Whoever it was, she knew what she was doing. I was looking in a cupboard under the sink when she came down on me like a ton of bricks." She touched her cheek. "I was out cold for a couple of minutes. When I came to, she was gone – and I found you."

"You saw her?"

"She was wearing a ski mask."

"The Filofax," Maddie said. "I found Paul's Filofax."

Tara shook her head. "It's not there now."

Maddie put her head in her hands. "She must have followed us," she said.

"I think she got what she wanted," Tara said. She took out her mobile. "I'm going to call for backup."

○

PIC Control.

Jack Cooper's office.

Simon Woods, the team leader of the GCHQ troubleshooting squad, sat in front of Jack Cooper's desk, sipping coffee, waiting while the boss of PIC read through the interim report.

"How soon can you have us up and running?" Cooper asked.

"Forty-eight hours," said Woods. He shrugged. "Maybe longer."

Jack Cooper frowned at him.

"You've been badly infected," Woods said, his eyebrows raising as he lifted the cup to his mouth. "And it was self-inflicted."

Cooper looked up at him. "You're sure about that?" he said.

Woods nodded. "The bouncing-bomb virus was introduced into the system using computer terminal PIC008MC. There's no doubt about it."

"That's my daughter's terminal," Cooper said. "Can you tell when the virus was introduced?"

"I'm afraid not. All I can tell you is that its activation would have been date and time specific," said Woods. "It could have sat there for half a year, waiting for the right moment to detonate. But it was introduced by someone with the username Swan Lake – is that your daughter?"

Jack Cooper nodded. "Could it have been introduced by someone who didn't realise what they were doing?"

"Highly unlikely," Woods said. "Your system is heavily protected. Someone would have had to override all the usual protocols to get it into the network." He looked at Jack Cooper. "Has anyone else been using your daughter's terminal? I noticed some recent documents on the hard drive under the name Kathryn Grant. She's not on your staff roll. Who is she?"

"You don't need to worry about her," Jack Cooper said.

Simon Woods took a sip of his coffee. "I take it your daughter is out of the frame."

"Absolutely," Jack Cooper said.

"In that case, you're looking for someone who has internal access to your daughter's terminal and who knows her username." He raised his eyebrows. "Do any particular people come to mind?"

"Several. And they're all people I trust." Jack Cooper leant forward in his wheelchair. "Let me get this absolutely clear. Are you telling me there's no doubt that the virus was put into the system by a member of my own staff?"

Simon Woods nodded. "PIC has a mole. If they're not flushed out pretty quickly, I'm going to have to report to the Home Secretary that your whole department is compromised – and that you should be shut down before even wider damage is caused."

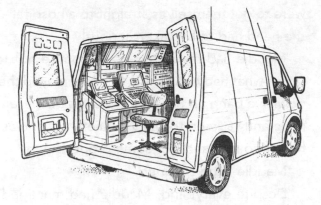

Chapter Fourteen

PIC Control.

The following day.

09:12.

Maddie and Tara were in Kevin Randal's office. He was reading Tara's report on the search of Paul Gilmore's flat.

Maddie was feeling rough, but she wasn't prepared to give in to it. The police doctor who had checked them over yesterday had found no serious damage, but he had sent them both home to rest and to recover from the attack. He had insisted that if they experienced any dizziness, nausea or double vision they were to get themselves straight to a hospital – blows to the head had to be taken seriously.

Maddie had made her gran promise not to tell her father what had happened. She had played the incident down – a bang on the head – no big deal. Her gran had reluctantly agreed to keep it quiet – so long as she took herself to bed and got some proper sleep.

Maddie hadn't argued.

Despite everything, Maddie had managed to sleep right through till morning.

There had been bad dreams. Paul – blood – fear. She had been glad when the morning had finally come to rescue her from the turmoil inside her head.

She had arrived at Control to find Tara already there. A flesh-coloured plaster covered the injury to her cheek.

DCI Randal wanted them in his office a.s.a.p.

Despite a nagging headache, Maddie was ready to get to work.

Kevin Randal finished reading Tara's report.

"So, we're dealing with a woman," he began. "That's progress, of a sort."

"I'm not so sure," Maddie said. "Paul mentioned a man. He said, 'The guy behind this is dangerous. He's got plans for you.' Those were his exact words."

"But at the Mercers Road flat you were jumped by a

woman," Kevin Randal said. "Where does that take us?"

"A man and a woman working together," Maddie suggested. "Or a woman working for a man."

Randal frowned. "According to your report, the woman dealt with both of you in a very professional way. She was quick, she was ruthless and she knew exactly what she was doing."

"I'd say she was an expert," Tara put in. "I didn't hear her until she was right on top of me – and she put me down with one blow." She touched the plaster on her cheek. "There aren't many people who can do that."

"Under normal circumstances," Randal said, "I'd get you to put a profile into the database and see what it throws up. But right now that's not an option. OK, lets run with this. What do we have? Version one: she was already at the flat when you got there. Version two: she followed you there. Either way, I think we can assume her target was Paul Gilmore's Filofax."

"Unless she took other stuff that we don't know about," Tara added. "I don't think Maddie had time to search the living room."

Maddie shook her head.

Kevin Randal looked at her. "It's a pity you didn't have time to take a look at the Filofax."

"I did," Maddie said. "Just for a moment. I remember a name – and an address."

Tara turned to Maddie, her eyes bright. "You didn't mention that."

Maddie nodded. "Pit Bull. Flat B... Hammersmith Grove." Her forehead creased. "I can't remember the house number." She looked at Randal. "Pit Bull was one of the names programmed into Paul's mobile phone."

Kevin Randal flicked through a pile of written reports. He nodded. "It's a mobile number. And no one is answering."

"Shall I start a door-to-door?" Tara asked. "Hammersmith Grove is a long road – it'll tie me up for at least a day."

"Let's see whether Maddie remembers the house number, first," Randal replied. "Anyway, the boss needs you, Tara – and I've got plenty of paperwork for you to be getting on with, Maddie."

○

Hammersmith Grove.

13:25.

Maddie brought her Vespa into the kerb. She took off her helmet and stared up at the large Victorian building.

568 Hammersmith Grove.

The house number had come back to her a few hours after the debrief with DCI Randal. She had been sorting and photocopying field reports when the much needed information came to her. It was tedious work which her computer could have done in a tenth of the time – if not for the fact that it was in pieces on her desk.

The IT team were swarming all over. The crisis of the previous day had turned into a long grind of laborious work. The only good news was that the GCHQ experts were now beginning to put it all back together again. Permanent damage had proven to be minimal – except in the financial sector. All the accounts for the past six months had been wiped.

Maddie's first thought had been to report the remembered house number to Kevin Randal, but he had been tied up in a meeting.

Danny was still out looking for Harvey Silver. Alex was up to his eyes in paperwork. Tara was with her father – not to be disturbed. There was no one to go with her to Hammersmith Grove.

She'd decided to do the job solo.

Hammersmith Grove was a long, dark street of tall Victorian houses. A mix of up-market one-family homes alongside run-down bedsits and student rental properties.

Number 568 was one of the cheap, run-down variety.

Maddie secured her motor scooter. She headed across the unkempt forecourt and up the flight of stone steps that led to the front door. There was a long row of bell pushes and a rusty intercom.

She checked the bell pushes. The house was divided into nine flats: A to I. Some of the bells had name tags. Flat B didn't.

She pressed and heard a distant, shrill ringing.

The intercom stayed silent. No one came to the door.

She went down the steps. The house was double fronted and semi-detached. She walked around to the side alley. There was a rough plank door. She moved a dustbin and climbed up, clinging to the door. Rotten wood crumbled away under her hands. The alley was an impassable tangle of junk and overgrown brambles. She'd need a machete to get through there.

She jumped back down. The jarring of her feet on the ground sent a sudden pain flaring through her head. In movies, people got over being knocked out in a couple of minutes. In real life, things weren't so easy.

Maddie began to have doubts. Maybe this wasn't such a good idea after all. What if she and Tara had been followed to Paul's flat – as DCI Randal had suggested – and what if the same woman was following her right now? She was on her own – and she wasn't exactly on top form.

She nursed her throbbing head, rubbing her temples. The truth was – the way she was feeling at that moment, she was pretty much a sitting duck.

○

PIC Control.

The Briefing Room.

Two hours earlier.

Jack Cooper had pulled in a team of his best field agents. The briefing was unusual. Very basic. The computer screens were blank. A hand-drawn map hung over the wall monitor.

The map was a blow-up of the Bermondsey area of southeast London. Tara had drawn the map on a large sheet of paper, using a Magic Marker. It was a world away from their usual computer-generated briefing devices. Slow – crude – painstaking. But it did the same job.

Jack Cooper was determined that PIC would continue its work. Operation Flatline was still running. It was vital that the chaos of the past few days did not undermine the effectiveness of ongoing cases.

New information had come in. This time, from three different sources. It needed an urgent response.

Danny and Alex were there. Kevin Randal was to lead the field team.

The map depicted a stretch of the Thames known as the Pool – a slow curve that reached from Tower Bridge on the left to Rotherhithe Tunnel on the right. Beneath it, running parallel to the river, was shown the line of Jamaica Road. Tara had also drawn in the network of streets that lay between the road and the river.

A red ring indicated the target zone.

"We have good reason to believe that a drugs laboratory is operating here, in a disused warehouse," Cooper informed his staff. They were making written notes. He glanced at Danny and Alex. "In the light of recent events, our information has been double-checked."

"Triple-checked would be good," Danny murmured. He lifted his pencil. "Wouldn't it be better if we held off on this for a few days, boss?" he asked. "We might find we could use a little computer backup when we hit the place."

Jack Cooper shook his head. "It's absolutely vital that PIC is shown to be open for business, despite all our current problems. That's why I'm not prepared to wait. I want no delays. No hesitation. This thing happens today." He looked at Kevin Randal. "We need to make good on this one, so use whatever resources you need." He scanned the room. "No more messing about. We need a result."

Chapter Fifteen

Maddie stood silently at the side of the house, watching the entrance to the forecourt, waiting for the throbbing in her head to subside. In her mind she saw a dark figure come creeping in from the road. Shadowing her. Waiting to pounce.

Her hands were trembling. She clenched them together, pushing her fears away. If people were out there gunning for her, then she would face them down. She'd fight back.

She walked to the stone steps again and climbed to the door. Methodically she began to ring the door bells.

Bell D produced a result.

The intercom crackled. An old voice spoke. "Who is it?"

Maddie put her mouth close to the rusty grill. "I'm sorry to disturb you," she said. "I'm trying to get in contact with the person who lives in flat B. Can you help me?"

"Wait there." There was another crackle, then the intercom fell silent.

Half a minute passed before an elderly man opened the door – small, stooped and very thin in baggy grey trousers and a green cardigan.

Maddie took out her PIC ID card. He peered at it for a few moments then stared at her.

"You look very young to be a policewoman," he said.

"I promise you I am one," Maddie said. "Could I ask you some questions about the person who lives in flat B?"

"I never could refuse a pretty face," the man said. "I'm Billy – I'm the caretaker. Would you like to come in? I can make us a nice cup of tea."

A few minutes later and Maddie was in a tiny living room, sitting on a shabby old armchair and holding a hot cup of tea, while Billy perched nearby on a dining chair.

"His name is Ian Dale," Billy told her. "He's only been here a few weeks. He seems a nice enough bloke. Always pays on the dot. Cash. Doesn't make any noise." He smiled. "I like a tenant like that. I like a quiet house."

"Did he give references when he moved in?" Maddie asked.

Billy chuckled. "I don't ask for references, dear. If a punter can stump up the deposit and four weeks rent in advance, that's good enough for me."

"Does he get much mail?" Maddie asked. "Many visitors?"

"No mail," Billy replied. "He must collect his social security money in person."

"What makes you think he's on social security?" Maddie asked.

"He certainly doesn't have a regular job," Billy told her. "Spends most of his time here. He only goes out now and then. He's got a lady friend – I can tell you that." Billy's eyes twinkled. "I hear her voice now and then. Never seen her, though."

"I rang his bell," Maddie said. "There was no answer. Has he gone out?"

"Now that you mention it, dear, I haven't heard a peep out of him for a couple of days. His flat is directly under mine, so I can usually hear the radio playing and whatever – but it's been quiet as the grave down there just lately."

Maddie didn't like the implications of that last remark.

"I don't have a search warrant so I can't officially go in there, but have you got duplicate keys?"

Billy nodded. "I've got keys for all the flats. What do you want him for? Something juicy? A bank robbery? An axe murder?"

Maddie winced. "He might be able to help us with our enquiries into a serious crime. That's all I can tell you."

"Serious, eh? Smashing!" Billy rubbed his hands together gleefully. "I like a bit of excitement." He stood up. "Shall we take a peek? No one needs to know." He went over to a dresser and pulled open a drawer. Maddie stood next to him. The drawer was full of tagged keys. Billy took a set. He grinned at her. "This is just like being on one of them telly cop shows. Do you think we'll find a dead body?"

Maddie shuddered.

They headed back down the stairs. Billy seemed quite taken with the idea of having a wanted criminal living below him. Maddie hardly even heard his ghoulish chatter. Her focus was on what might lie behind the closed door of flat B.

○

Bermondsey, SE16.

13:40.

Kevin Randal had got his troops into position.

It was almost time to move.

The warehouse was one of several that faced each other across an empty forecourt. The whole place seemed abandoned. There were a couple of skips. A disintegrating car. Broken windows.

It was a good place for the manufacture of illegal drugs – tucked out of sight, unused. Awaiting demolition.

Danny was with the main team – watching the front entrance. Waiting for the word.

Alex was at the back. He had the four agents with him. They had climbed over walls to get there. The windows were guarded by thick black metal bars. But there was a precarious-looking metal stairway up to a high door. That was to be their way in.

Kevin Randal was wearing a headset. He was staring at his watch. The second hand swept up to the twelve. "OK," he said. "Let's do it."

Danny ran with the others to the front of the

warehouse. There were huge wooden gates. A smaller doorway had been cut into one of them. One man held a power ram. There was a crash as the ram hit the door. It buckled. Splinters flew. At the second stroke, the door crumpled.

PIC agents poured into the warehouse.

At the back, a similar scene was taking place. Alex had the ram. He hammered it into the metal door, focusing the power near the lock. It took four blows before the door gave.

"We're in," he said into his face mike.

There were armed agents at his back.

Whatever they found in there, they would be able to deal with it.

This time PIC were going to strike gold.

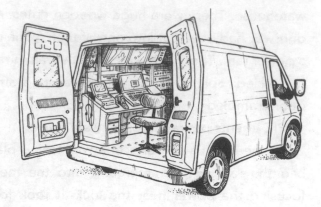

Chapter Sixteen

568 Hammersmith Grove.

13:50.

Billy opened the door. He stepped back and grinned at Maddie.

"After you, dear," he said. "Just in case there's a mad axe-man hiding in the bathroom."

Not funny.

Maddie stepped into a small entrance area. The place smelled faintly unpleasant. A tiny kitchen led off to the right. She opened a door. The living room was shabby. The window was shrouded with grimy net curtains. The furniture was old and worn.

Maddie looked around the room. There were no personal items – nothing to show that anyone lived there.

She turned and walked through to the kitchen. Dirty pots, plates and cutlery were piled into cold water in the sink. The cooker was greasy. She opened the fridge. There was a carton of milk. A slab of butter in a foil wrap.

A narrow corridor led to the bedroom. A desk stood in front of drawn curtains. Maddie walked across and threw the curtains open. French windows led to the overgrown garden.

"Looks like he's done a bunk," Billy said, rubbing his hands together. "I'll have to put another ad in the newsagents window." He frowned. "He paid up to the end of the month. They usually do a flit owing rent – not the other way around."

The room certainly showed all the signs of a hasty exit. Drawers hung open. The wardrobe door gaped. The bed was unmade.

Maddie went past Billy, turning off into the bathroom which also had the look of a place hastily abandoned. She took thin latex gloves out of her shoulder bag and drew them on. She crouched and looked into a plastic waste bin by the sink. There was a discarded razor. Some cotton wool balls. She picked one up between finger and

145

thumb. It had been used to clean off make-up.

Ian Dale's lady friend, presumably.

She went into the living room.

Billy grinned again and winked conspiratorially. "Looks like he knew you were coming, dear."

Maddie looked at him. Was that possible? Had Pit Bull heard of Paul's murder and done a runner? Or was he more intimately involved than that?

Either way, Maddie had seen all there was to see here.

"I'll need the keys," she said. "This place has to be locked up till our forensic team arrives." She gave a final glance around the room. There was something behind the couch. A flash of colour. She crouched and picked the thing up.

It was a lime-green voile scarf. A woman's scarf – forgotten in the rush to leave the flat.

Maddie held the scarf to her face. She frowned – the scent was familiar. She breathed in, trying to remember where she had smelt it before, but the memory escaped her. She laid the scarf over the back of the armchair.

"He had a little fire out back the day before yesterday," Billy said suddenly. "I almost forgot. I had to close my windows 'cos of the smoke. He was burning paper."

"Show me," Maddie said.

Danny stepped through the broken doorway. Agents who had gone in ahead of him were raking the large room with flashlight beams. There were shelves – pallets – heaped rubbish. No signs of occupation.

A side door opened at the back of the empty expanse. Light spilled out. A face stared.

"Police!" shouted Kevin Randal. "Stop right where you are!"

They converged on the doorway. A young woman stood there – her eyes wide with shock. She had long hair and she was wearing a brocaded dress that reached to her sandaled feet.

"What do you want?" she gasped.

"Where are the rest of you?" Randal asked.

Her voice shook. "Upstairs. I don't understand."

"Cuff her," Randal said. He pushed past the woman. Danny looked at her – she seemed completely bewildered.

Alex was the first into the upstairs room. It was at the end of a darkened corridor. It was lit by candles and filled with the smoky scent of incense sticks.

A dozen or so people were sitting cross-legged on the floor. They had their eyes closed – they were humming softly and melodically. At one end of the room a tapestry showed a long-haired, bearded man – floating cross-legged in space above a picture of the planet earth. There was an arc of silver spaceships around his head.

The startled ring of people broke up as the PIC team burst in.

Alex stared around the room. Weird music was playing – like whale song put through a synthesiser.

There was no sign of drugs-making paraphernalia.

Alex spoke into his microphone. "We've found them." He looked at the alarmed faces of the people they had discovered. "But... I'm not too sure about this."

✪

The French windows opened into brambles. Someone had passed that way recently – the branches had been pushed aside and trampled. Maddie gestured for Billy to stay back.

A few metres down the garden was a clear patch in the undergrowth. A buckled and blackened incinerator bin stood over a pile of ash. Maddie picked up a stick. She stirred the pile. White dust rose. There were pieces of charred stuff – mostly shards of wood used to fuel the fire.

Maddie crouched and trawled her fingers through the ash.

Nothing.

She stood up. There was more half-burnt stuff in the bin. She tipped it over and upended it. Clouds of smoke billowed around her. She coughed, throwing the incinerator bin down and pushing it out of the way with her foot.

She waited for the dust to settle.

"Found anything?" Billy called from the French windows.

"Not yet. Stay there," Maddie called back.

She crouched again. Some of the embers were still warm – the fire must have burnt itself out over a long period. She searched the pile of ash.

She found a section of a badly-burnt spiral-bound notebook. She opened the fragile, cracking pages. The fire had scorched it beyond her ability to read anything that meant anything to her. But then something caught her eye – a scribble on a fragment of paper that had escaped the flames.

... of the Jeweller's Sh...

The Jeweller's Shop, she presumed – whatever that meant. She could just make out numbers – a column of figures with pound signs in front of them. Someone had been adding up sums of money. She took a small plastic evidence pouch from her bag and slipped the notebook inside, sealing it along the top with her fingers.

She continued the search. A lot of paper had been burnt, but nothing else was salvageable. As she stood up, something caught her eye at the edge of the clearing.

She stooped and picked it up. It was a laminated card – half consumed by the fire. An ID card – not unlike her own.

There was a photo of a man's face, and a name. DCI Ian Dowd.

A cold sensation flooded her stomach. She knew that name.

DCI Dowd was a Special Branch officer – he had nearly wrecked a PIC operation in Essex a couple of months ago.

The name of Billy's tenant was Ian Dale – the name on the ID card was Ian Dowd. It was the same man – it had to be.

But what was DCI Dowd's ID pass doing here? And how did it link to the murder of Paul Gilmore?

Maddie had come here looking for answers – she had found more questions instead.

Chapter Seventeen

Sky TV News.

15.00.

An outside report from Bermondsey.

A well-groomed man in a light grey suit. Jason Brand.

Behind him, deserted warehouses faced each other across an empty forecourt. There were a couple of over-filled rubbish skips. A rusted and collapsing car. Broken windows.

Jason Brand was speaking.

"Only a few hours ago, a squad of police officers broke into the warehouse that you can see way down there on the left." He half turned to indicate it. The gates were closed, but a black rectangle could be seen where the small door had been. "They were acting on information that it was being used as an illegal drugs laboratory. But their intelligence proved to be badly mistaken. The warehouse was, in fact, being rented by a man known to his followers as Shaka Ramses Jones. For the past five years Mr Jones has been the spiritual leader of a New Age religious group who call themselves The Children of Rialma Veda. They were at their devotions when a large group of armed police officers burst into the building and held them at gunpoint.

"Several arrests were made, including that of Mr Jones. A police spokesman stated that thirteen people in total had been helping the police with their enquiries, but that all the detainees had subsequently been released without charge.

"The spokesman was unable to comment on questions about heavy-handed police tactics or on the cost of such a botched operation. We were told that a full report of the incident would be available at a later date.

"This is Jason Brand, reporting to you from Bermondsey."

A TV Studio.

A woman was speaking. Zena Omar – co-host of a 24/7 news programme. At her back was a blow-up of the Metropolitan Police shield, next to a portrait of a middle-aged woman with an intelligent face and piercing eyes.

"Margaret Churchill became Home Secretary just a few weeks ago with the promise that she would overhaul the Met and make sure that the public not only got value for money, but that elite departments such as the shadowy Police Investigation Command would be made more accountable," Zena Omar was saying. "Sources close to the Home Secretary have suggested that recent problems with the Home Office computer network have been traced to a virus introduced into the system at the headquarters of this secretive department. Police Investigation Command was also behind the costly and mishandled raid on a harmless group of British citizens today. Questions are now being asked about whether this particular sub-division of the Met should be disbanded."

PIC Control.

The Briefing Room.

15:12.

The PIC computer network was up and running. The GCHQ team had pieced together the entire Cobra plexus. More than ninety per cent of the archived data had been retrieved, but the mood at Control was far from celebratory.

Zena Omar's face was frozen on the wall monitor. Jack Cooper put down the remote control and turned to look out across the crowded room. All available staff were there – summoned on short notice to an emergency briefing.

There was an ominous atmosphere in the room.

Maddie Cooper watched her father's face. It was unreadable, as ever, but she understood enough to know the emotions that must be gnawing at him. Jack Cooper disliked publicity at the best of times. PIC could not function under a spotlight. This publicity was not simply unwelcome – it was potentially catastrophic.

Jack Cooper spoke quietly but precisely, his voice penetrating every corner of the room.

"I don't need to tell you how serious the situation has become," he said, "but I do need to inform you of the direct consequences of our most recent problem." He took a breath. "I have just spoken to the Home Secretary on the phone. She has ordered the complete suspension of PIC, pending an investigation of the raid."

"She can't do that," said a voice. "We have to fight back, boss."

Jack Cooper's eyes blazed. "The Home Secretary is an elected Member of Parliament, appointed to her post by the Prime Minister. She is my direct superior, and all decisions concerning this department are in her hands."

Alex stood up. "Are you saying we stand down?" he asked. "She's using us as scapegoats. All she's interested in is cutting her budget."

"The Home Secretary is not our enemy," said Jack Cooper. "But she does get the final word." He frowned. "I'm not suggesting we all pack our bags and go home, but we do have to accept the realities of the situation."

"I don't buy it," Danny said. "So we made a couple of bad busts – it doesn't make sense to close us down for something like that. Is there something you know that we don't, boss?"

Jack Cooper smiled. "I can't begin to tell you how much I know that you don't know, Danny," he said, with a rare flash of gallows humour. "But I will say this – there are reasons behind the Home Secretary's decision that I am currently not at liberty to reveal. An investigation into this department is currently under way which may very well shut us down for good."

A murmur ran through the room.

Maddie looked at Danny and Alex. This had come out of the blue. PIC was in deeper trouble than any of them had imagined.

"As of now, the majority of you are suspended on full pay," Jack Cooper continued. "Tara has the list of who is to remain at Control. I have one last thing to say – I'm going to fight this thing. PIC will survive. Dismissed."

○

PIC Control.

The Briefing Room.

17:00.

The offices of Control were eerily quiet. Only a skeleton staff remained. Jack Cooper and Tara were there. Section Head Kevin Randal was one of the few – along with Maddie, Danny, Alex and a thin scattering of agents needed to keep things ticking over.

There was only one item on the agenda: Maddie's report on her visit to Hammersmith Grove.

Jack Cooper had invited an outsider to attend the debrief – a high-ranking Special Branch officer: Detective Superintendent Michael Preston.

For his benefit, Maddie ran through the whole story – beginning with her first encounter with Paul Gilmore at Cloud Nine. DS Preston listened with silent attention, making occasional notes as she brought her report up to date with her finds in the back garden of 568 Hammersmith Grove.

She sat down.

Jack Cooper looked at their Special Branch guest. "Well, Superintendent – can you shed any light on why DCI Dowd's Identity Card was there?"

DS Preston nodded. "I think I can," he said. "But first of all, I'd like to explain the entry that Agent Cooper found in the notebook. The reference to the Jeweller's Shop. That's Special Branch code for the Gems laboratory. We know that it's located in London, but we've had no luck pinning it down to a particular address. Ian Dowd was working on the case. He knew a great deal more about the enterprise than he ever put into any of his reports." He paused for a moment. "DCI Dowd was sacked from Special Branch two months ago."

"This was after he interfered with Operation Snake Pit, I assume?" Jack Cooper asked.

"It was an internal matter," replied DS Preston. "He wasn't let go because of his unauthorised actions in Essex – he was thrown out for gross insubordination."

Maddie had been intimately involved in Operation

Snake Pit. It had centred around a motorway hotel in Harlow. PIC had been staking out a summit meeting of UK crime bosses – keeping a low profile – watching how events unfolded. Ian Dowd and his team had gone blundering into the middle of the operation, allowing many of the crooks to escape and very nearly wrecking the whole operation. It was all in the report. But there was no mention of what had happened to Dowd after the event. His sacking was news to everyone in the room.

DS Preston continued. "Ian Dowd was a clever man and potentially a very promising police officer – but he had opinions that he would have been better off keeping to himself." He looked at Jack Cooper. "At the disciplinary hearing convened to investigate his actions in Harlow, he let it be known that he had reasons for a personal dislike of you, Chief Superintendent."

Maddie looked at her father. More revelations.

"He put in an application last year to join PIC," Jack Cooper said. "He was rejected. I get several dozen applications a month. The vast majority are rejected. Dowd had no reason to feel slighted."

"Nevertheless, he did," said DS Preston. "And I believe his intervention in Operation Snake Pit was a misguided attempt to show you that he was worth your better opinion."

"Behaviour like that would only have confirmed my original decision. The man was not PIC material." Jack Cooper looked at DS Preston. "I hope Special Branch will not take offence at that comment."

"Not at all," said DS Preston. "PIC requires very specific skills and I agree – Dowd didn't have them."

"So what happened after he got the boot?" Danny asked.

"A great deal happened," DS Preston said. "After his sacking, it became obvious that Dowd had been helping himself to the drugs picked up in our investigations and held as evidence."

There was silence in the room. DS Preston had everyone's full attention.

"He was selling the drugs through a network of pushers," DS Preston continued. "He'd carved out quite a lucrative empire for himself." He frowned. "Dowd was trusted and we didn't monitor his activities carefully enough. That's a mistake we won't be making again."

"He must have known you'd find out that he was skimming off the top once you'd sacked him," said Alex. "I imagine he did a runner, yes?"

DS Preston nodded. "We've been searching for him ever since." He looked at Maddie. "You seem to have come the closest – it sounds like you only missed him by a day or so. Our investigations show that Pit Bull was the alias he used with his pushers. The dead boy – Paul Gilmore – he was one of them."

"A picture is beginning to emerge," said Jack Cooper. "We have a renegade ex-Special Branch officer with a grudge against both myself and PIC. This man has had access to a large stock of drugs and presumably filled his pockets before he was dismissed. Linked to him we have a pusher named Paul Gilmore, who was told to plant both drugs and money on my daughter."

"I'll tell you what else we have," said Danny. "We have one of my best informants suddenly feeding me garbage about a big drugs deal and we have formerly reliable people sending us off on a wild goose chase to strong-arm a bunch of harmless tree-hugging hippies."

Alex nodded. "I agree with Danny – this is all linked," he said. "Dowd has gone down and now he's trying to take us down with him."

"But Dowd isn't on his own," Maddie said. "There's a woman helping him." She glanced at Tara. "The woman who attacked us at the Holloway flat must be the same woman who visited Dowd at Hammersmith Grove." She looked at DS Preston. "Was Dowd married?"

"No," he said. "But we do know he had a long-term girlfriend. None of his colleagues had ever met her or knew anything about her, except for one thing – they were pretty sure that the girlfriend was also in the police."

"In Special Branch?" Kevin Randal asked.

"I think not," Jack Cooper said. "I have something to tell you that mustn't go beyond these four walls." He looked at DS Preston. The Special Branch officer gave a curt nod. "The interim report by the Home Secretary's IT team has concluded that the bouncing-bomb virus was introduced into our system deliberately and with full knowledge of the consequences." He looked at the stunned faces around him. "I believe that the virus was introduced by someone on my own staff. DS Preston's report – coupled with what Maddie has told us of her finds at Hammersmith Grove – gives me reason to believe that the person who crashed our computers is Ian Dowd's girlfriend." He looked around at his PA. "Thirty-seven female agents work in this building. I have asked Tara to begin a full investigation into every one of them, with the sole exception of my daughter."

"Is Susan Baxendale included in the investigation?" Kevin Randal asked.

"She is," Jack Cooper said. "At this point, I'm afraid

I can't even eliminate DCI Baxendale from suspicion."
His eyes gleamed with anger. "This woman has got to
be found."

Chapter Eighteen

PIC Control.

17:52.

There were only six agents left at Control.

Jack Cooper was with Tara Moon in his top-floor office. They were trying to get to grips with the fallout of the Bermondsey disaster. Kevin Randal was at the Comms Desk, fending off unwanted media calls and keeping a lid on things. Maddie, Danny and Alex were struggling at a computer terminal – they had been given the task of tracking down the Jeweller's Shop.

It was not proving easy.

They had made some progress and Danny was firing on all cylinders: full of inspiration. It was complex and convoluted stuff and there were times when Maddie and Alex were only clinging to his thought processes by their fingertips.

They pulled up the forensic breakdown of the chemical constituents of Gems. Then they searched for manufacturers and synthesisers of these elements, using the Internet as their front-line tool – following every thread. They listed chemical distributors – importers and exporters. They downloaded information on transportation and scheduling, payments and deliveries. They worked out the notarised trafficking of everything from benzyl methyl ketone to phenylnitropropene and beyond.

It all needed to be logged and cross-referenced. Decisions had to be made as to what was relevant and what was useless. A single mistake meant a lot of lost time while they back-tracked and picked up a discarded thread.

But gradually the bulk of data was being reduced. Instead of 23,416 files they were down to just a few hundred. But still they were unable to make sense of what they were finding.

Danny was lying on the floor, his arms crossed over

his face – hoping the darkness would help him to concentrate – to allow him to pull some new ideas out of his head.

Alex was seething with dammed-up frustration. He stalked the empty office, shouting out suggestions to Maddie as they flashed into his mind.

Maddie was at the computer. Her head was aching. There were discarded plastic coffee cups on the desk. She felt like her brain was hot-wired with caffeine. Things were beginning to get fuzzy around the edges. She was waiting for someone to have a fresh idea that would move the whole thing on.

She looked around at Danny. He was muttering to himself.

"We're so close," she said. "What are we missing?"

"About ten billion brain cells," Danny said. He sighed and sat up. "What have we got so far?"

Alex stared at the screen. "Three hundred and seventy-two possible addresses in the Greater London area."

"OK," Danny said. "Maddie – log on to the Companies Directory – find out which of those addresses are registered. That should take a few out."

The long search recommenced.

19:05.

Maddie stared at the screen – hardly able to believe what she was seeing.

Danny was leaning on her shoulder – Alex was standing over them.

The cross wires had finally intermeshed on a single address: Unit 17, Blixa Industrial Estate, Camden Lock, NW1.

Alex snatched up a phone and punched Jack Cooper's number.

Tara answered.

"Tell the boss we've got it," Alex said.

There was a moment's pause, then Jack Cooper's voice sounded down the phone.

"Are you completely sure about this, Alex?" he asked.

Alex put his hand over the phone. "He wants to know if we're one hundred per cent."

Danny grinned up at him, all that brain-shredding work swept away by the euphoria of success. "Tell him I'm one hundred and ten per cent!" he said.

Maddie stared at the screen, her eyes bleary from hours of effort. "Now what?" she murmured.

Danny opened a celebratory pack of M&Ms. "Now," he said, "we shut 'em down."

PIC Control.

Jack Cooper's office.

22:00.

Jack Cooper had called back a very select group of PIC agents. He had a job for them to do. They were gathered in his office – ten experienced field agents, along with DCI Randal, Maddie, Danny and Alex.

Jack Cooper was sitting with his back to the night-time panorama of London. Tara stood at his side. The city below was alive with points of white light.

"If this operation is successful, "Jack Cooper said. "There's a chance that PIC will survive. If it fails, we'll be closed down. There's no margin for error. You're my best people. Go out there and get it right."

"And if we don't?" Danny whispered to Alex.

"We look for new jobs," Alex whispered back.

"OK!" Jack Cooper said. "We'll go over the details one more time, and then we're done."

❂

The Blixa Industrial Estate, Camden Lock.

23:12.

The MSU was parked a couple of streets away from the estate. Alex had gone in solo with night-vision goggles, an infrared camera and a throat mike. Kevin

Randal sat at Danny's side in the cramped back of the van, listening to his report and watching the on-screen feed from the camera.

The industrial estate was a row of modern units backing on to the railway. There was no sign of activity. Alex swept the camera around – giving the watchers in the MSU a clear idea of the terrain. Tarmac access roads – open forecourts. Not much in the way of cover.

Alex slipped between two of the units and made his way to the back.

He kept down, moving cautiously.

"Don't get too close, Alex," Randal said into his mike.

"It's cool," Alex said. The unsteady picture on-screen showed that he was moving nearer to Unit 17.

"Do you see any sign of activity?" Danny asked.

"Not from here."

"Take no chances," Randal said. "We don't want to spook them."

Alex moved along the back of the units. "There's light coming from a window at the back of Unit 17," he said.

The infrared picture edged around a corner. The light flared on-screen – amplified by the camera's array of heat-sensitive photo detectors.

"Someone's putting in some overtime," Danny murmured. "Watch yourself, Alex."

"Got it."

The continuing movement of the camera picked up two cars parked alongside the unit.

"This is as close as I can get," Alex said. "Unless you want me to go and say hi."

"Pull back," said Kevin Randal. "I'll get the team together."

He stepped out of the MSU. The ten agents gathered around him.

A few seconds later, Alex appeared.

"We're going in," Randal said. "Let's make this a good one."

✪

PIC Control.

Jack Cooper sat alone at his desk. Tara had gone down to cover the Comms Desk. The solitude suited his mood.

It was at times like this that his disability weighed most heavily on him. If not for his useless legs, he would have been out there with his agents instead of sitting in his office and waiting for news.

The main light was off. He was working by the light of a halogen desk lamp, reading documents, making notes in the margins. Keeping his mind occupied. Faint street sounds drifted up – the growl of buses along Charing Cross Road. The occasional car horn. Traffic noises from way below, emphasising the unnatural silence that surrounded him.

Jack Cooper was only too well aware of the risk he had taken. He had given the operation in Camden Lock the go-ahead without official sanction. If something went wrong, his career would be over.

The thought of that broke Jack Cooper's concentration. He turned his chair and wheeled himself over to the broad window. He gazed out across the city – looking towards the bright hoop of the London Eye. He glanced at his watch. Kevin Randal should be leading his troops into battle right about now.

He heard a stifled sound from behind him. He half-turned. From the corner of his eye, he caught sight of something dark coming down towards his head.

A blinding pain filled his skull and he passed out.

Chapter Nineteen

Kevin Randal split his forces into two teams. Standard tactics: five agents to effect an entry through the front – five more in through the back. The two remaining agents were put out on point duty on the road with orders to report any incoming activity. Maddie was one of them.

She crouched alone in the darkness on the far side of the road. She was shielded behind a low brick wall, watching the road and listening on her headset as the raid teams got into their final positions. Her orders were to report anything: cars – pedestrians – any movement at all.

She stared into the darkness between the streetlights – watching shadows – hyper-alert.

Something caught her attention. There was a gap between walls to her left – some distance away from the unit. A narrow alley or gateway. Deep in black shade. But the edge of the shadow was not straight. It was contoured – uneven.

Maddie strained her eyes, her heart beginning to beat a little faster. She couldn't be sure, but it almost looked as if there was something – or someone – pressing against the wall over there.

Through her headset she heard DCI Randal give the order to go.

This was not a good time to report a vague sighting. She needed to get confirmation.

She slipped away from her post and ran in a silent crouch along the road, keeping close in under the wall, coming gradually towards the dark gap.

She stopped a metre or so away. She switched her headset off and listened intently for any tell-tale sounds. For a few moments there was nothing. Then she heard a soft, mocking voice – no more than a whisper in the night.

"Hello, Maddie."

Her heart pounding, she moved out into the open.

"Who is that?" she said. "Come out where I can see you."

A figure slid smoothly out of the black alley. There was a whiff of a familiar perfume.

Maddie stared at the smiling woman. "Tara?" Confusion filled her mind. "Why aren't you with my father?"

The smile vanished from Tara's face. She leapt at Maddie, her hand rose and fell in a blur of movement. Maddie tried to ward the blow off, but the force drove her to her knees.

Tara was on her in an instant.

Maddie was thrown on to her back as Tara's full weight came down on her.

Her arm rose again and her hand came scything down towards Maddie's neck in a killing karate chop.

✪

Jack Cooper woke up into a world of pain. He was lying on the floor in his office. His upturned wheelchair was beside him.

He was not alone. Someone was cradling him – holding a glass to his lips.

"Drink," a voice said.

He felt a cold edge against his lips. He drank. It was water. He was vaguely aware of a strange aftertaste.

"That's the idea," said the voice. "Just a little more." He drank more as the glass was tipped. He coughed. Water ran from the sides of his mouth.

"There you go," said the voice. "That should do it." His vision began to clear. He struggled to get up.

"Now, now, keep calm," said the voice. Jack Cooper looked up. A face hung in the air above him. He blinked and tried to focus. The face swam into clear sight.

Cooper recognised the man in an instant. It was Ian Dowd. He was smiling – but his eyes were dead.

"Not hurt too badly, I hope?" Dowd said. He heaved Jack Cooper up and propped him against the wall. Jack Cooper watched him in silence – desperately trying to assess the situation.

Dowd turned Jack Cooper's wheelchair the right way up and wheeled it to the desk. He sat in it and began to type. Cooper saw that he was opening an Internet link.

"So, this is what it feels like to be the great Jack Cooper," Dowd said. "Lord of Police Investigation Command. Emperor of all he surveys." His voice was soft but filled with menace. "You should have given me a job, you know. That was all I wanted. It would have saved you all this unpleasantness."

Cooper tried to lift himself.

"Don't move," Dowd said. He drew a gun from his jacket pocket and pointed it down at Cooper. He smiled. "I took this when they sacked me. I thought it might come in useful." He frowned. "Why the sulky silence? Aren't you dying to know why I'm here?"

Jack Cooper stared at him.

Dowd broke eye contact quickly. He laughed. "I hope you enjoyed that drink," he said. "It contained quite a large number of powdered Gems. More than the manufacturer's recommended dosage, I'm afraid. But I don't want to have to shoot you before they kick in – so keep still and be patient. I've got some important work to do while we're waiting."

Cooper said nothing. He was trying to gauge Dowd's mental state. Angry? Agitated? Mad?

"What – no questions?" Dowd said. "You're going to spoil it for me. But I'll let you know what I've got planned, all the same. It's only fair – and you'll appreciate it, I'm sure."

He opened an email file. "Time to get busy," he said.

His voice sounded unnaturally calm. Cooper found that more disturbing than if Dowd had been ranting.

Dowd opened a new message file and typed in the address box: **Home Secretary**. Then he moved the cursor down to the main body of the letter.

He glanced around at Cooper. "Can you see OK?" he asked. "I don't want you to miss anything."

Dowd typed:

Madam,

I have been systematically embezzling funds from this department for many months. No one else on my staff has been involved and I take full responsibility for my criminal activities.

Dowd turned his head and smiled again. "Like it so far?"

My actions have irreversibly compromised the security of this department and I therefore recommend that PIC be disbanded with immediate effect.

Dowd turned again. "Now for the best part of all." A flicker of hatred came and went in his face. "The big goodbye."

I regret that I cannot live with the shame of my actions.

DCS Jack Cooper.

It was as Dowd typed in his name that Jack Cooper felt the first effects of the drugs. The room seemed to pulse in and out. Lines and angles blurred and melted. The words on the screen became an indecipherable black swirl.

He lunged forwards, using all his upper-body strength to try to pull Dowd down out of the chair.

Dowd spun the chair and lashed out with his foot. Jack Cooper was thrown back against the wall, winded by the blow to his chest.

"Sit where you are and be a good boy," Dowd said. He leant towards Cooper, the calm beginning to crack – anger and bitter hatred filling his face. "Did you think we were going to let you get to the truth about who's been siphoning all the money off?" he spat.

Jack Cooper gasped for breath. Dowd's face looked like something out of a nightmare – distorting and changing as Cooper tried to fight the effects of the drugs. He filled his lungs for a desperate cry. "Tara!" His skin was crawling, his face beaded with sweat.

"She isn't here," Dowd hissed. "Not that it would do you much good if she was." He leant in closer. "Haven't you worked it out yet?" he said. "It was Tara who was taking the money – stealing it right out from under your stupid nose."

Cooper wasted his ebbing strength on a last attempt to pull Dowd down. But it was useless. Dowd pressed the heel of his shoe into Cooper's chest and pushed him down on to the floor.

"Feeling bad?" he asked. "That's what happens

when you overdose on Gems." He grabbed Cooper and dragged him up into a sitting position again. "Not that you need worry too much about the long-term effects," he said. "You'll be cooked meat a long time before the drugs could kill you."

He turned back to the desk, bringing his hand down over the mouse. He moved the cursor to the Send icon. He clicked and the email vanished off the screen. It showed for a few moments in the Outbox section. Then it was gone.

Dowd laughed.

Cooper tried to speak but his tongue felt thick and heavy in his mouth. He could not form words – he could hardly think. He watched helplessly as Dowd stood up and walked around the desk. He stooped and lifted a grip-bag up on to the desk.

Dowd opened it, his face impassive as he worked. He lifted a black box out of the grip and placed it under Cooper's desk. He flipped a switch on the top and a small red light began to blink.

Dowd stood up, coming around the desk again and staring down at Cooper for a few moments. He crouched, his fingers gripping under Cooper's chin, holding his lolling head so that they were eye-to-eye.

"Still with me, Chief Superintendent?" he sneered.

"I hope so, because I want you to hear this."

Jack Cooper made an attempt to speak, but his words came out garbled.

"Good. You're still in there," said Dowd. "Now, listen carefully. I want to tell you where Tara is. She's in Camden. Are you listening? She's being a very busy girl right now. I've sent her on a special mission." His fingers dug into Jack Cooper's face. "I want this to be the last thing you think about before you die, Cooper – my lovely, wonderful red-haired sweetheart is going to kill your daughter."

Chapter Twenty

Maddie's arm came up instinctively, blocking the full force of Tara's karate chop. The woman's face was livid with anger. Maddie knew she had to act quickly – Tara was a formidable opponent.

Tara's arm rose again, this time ready to bring her fist pounding down into Maddie's face.

Maddie snatched hold of Tara's collar. She heaved upwards – throwing Tara off balance – tipping her forwards over her head.

Now that Tara's weight was off her, Maddie was able to twist around. She brought her legs sweeping around to drag Tara's arms away and send her crashing on to her face. Maddie sprang up, coming down hard on Tara's back. She snatched at her leg, bending it up, trying to form an ankle-lock.

But Tara was too quick. She slithered away and bounced up on to her feet.

Maddie staggered up, spreading her legs, getting a good footing – awaiting the charge.

Tara ducked down and drove her shoulder into Maddie's midriff, throwing her arms around Maddie's waist and trying to push her off balance.

As she felt herself falling, Maddie hooked her arm under Tara's and twisted – rolling Tara over and bringing her down. She brought her leg over and leant back. Even at such a time, a voice in her head told her to go easy – she had Tara in a lock that could break her neck.

Tara took advantage of Maddie's hesitation. She slid out of the lock, panting and wild-eyed.

The two of them backed off for a second – then came together at speed. Maddie hardly knew what was happening as Tara launched a series of punches and kicks. Maddie fended them off, but she was driven gradually back by the ferocity of the attack.

She spun, delivering a high kick, sending Tara reeling. She followed through, attempting a double-leg take down – still just trying to immobilise Tara – still not understanding why she had been attacked. She secured her grip around Tara's legs. She drove her feet into the ground, pushing Tara back.

Tara reached down and caught Maddie in a front choke – her arm locking around her neck – her hands clasped to secure the grip.

Maddie felt the forearm tighten against her windpipe. She knew she was in real danger now, but there was nothing she could do. Tara leant back, bringing Maddie helplessly down. Tara's legs wrapped around her – holding her in place.

Tara's arm tightened around Maddie's neck – choking her – disorientating her. Black flashes distorted her vision. She began to lose consciousness.

Tara shifted position, forcing Maddie down, keeping her neck in a vice-like grip, bringing her mouth close to Maddie's ear. "Don't worry," she whispered sharply. "I'll make it quick. You won't suffer like your dad."

A glimmer of awareness awoke in Maddie's brain.

"First he'll go crazy – then he'll burn. What do you think? Is that enough payback for ruining Ian's life?"

Anger gave Maddie a final rush of strength. Tara had made the mistake of gloating before she had finished the job.

Maddie gripped her hands, forcing them to loosen, wrenching them back. Tara gave a cry of pain as Maddie bent her hand down against the joint. The pressure was off Maddie's neck. She could breathe again. She squirmed free, catching her balance – holding Tara on the ground. No more compassion. She had to finish this thing.

Maddie centred herself for a split second. She released Tara's hand and spun. She lashed out with her foot, delivering a perfect *mawashi geri* – a devastating roundhouse kick.

Tara's head snapped back and she crumpled to the ground.

Maddie stood panting over her. She fought down an overwhelming desire to keep on hitting the fallen woman. If she succumbed to feelings like that, she was no better than her enemy.

She lifted her head, staring up into the sky and sucking in much-needed air.

Then she knelt and touched her fingers against Tara's neck. There was a wild pulse. She turned Tara on to her side. There was blood where her head had hit the ground.

Maddie stood up. She swayed. Dizzy.

Her headset had broken in the fight.

She stumbled across the road towards the industrial units.

○

The raid had been successful. The PIC agents had smashed their way in – finding the Gems laboratory working at full capacity and taking the drugs makers completely by surprise. The shocked workers had gone belly up in the first fifteen seconds.

As Maddie ran towards Unit 17, people were already being brought out in handcuffs, heads down, shuffling along.

Maddie wiped her arm across her eyes – trying to get her head together. Alex was there, by the doors, shepherding the captives through. She almost stumbled into him.

He caught hold of her. His eyes were bright with concern. "What?"

The words tumbled out of her – Tara – back there – and her father – in trouble – at Control – no time. Must get to him.

"Stay here," he said. "I'll deal with it."

"No!" Maddie caught his arm as he broke away from her. "I'm coming too."

Alex looked at her for a moment – then nodded.

They ran side by side to where he had parked his

Ducati. He snatched helmets out of the pillion box, helping her into hers and strapping it tight.

She climbed on behind him, clinging to him as he started the motor.

Moments later, they were speeding south down Camden High Street – heading for Centre Point.

Ian Dowd walked across the open forecourt of Centre Point. St Giles Circus still teemed with life – activity didn't end at midnight in this part of town. Cars and taxis cruised by. Pedestrians, alone or in laughing groups, walked the pavements. Neon signs and shop lights shone out brightly.

Dowd held the grip-bag tightly as he walked towards his car. It was almost empty now. He had been busy. He pressed the remote as he came near to his car. The lights flashed three times. He opened the door and stepped inside.

He sat quietly for a few moments – savouring the events of the last half hour.

Sweet revenge.

He took a triggering device out of the bag. A small black box that fitted across his two open palms. There were dials. He adjusted them carefully. As he turned the final dial, a small red light ignited. The mechanism was primed and ready.

He leant sideways and looked up at the immense white tower of Centre Point.

He smiled as he brought his thumb down on to the red detonation button.

○

A black box rested on the table in the Briefing Room – its red light winking on and off. There was a barely-audible click. A wisp of smoke rose from the box. A few seconds passed. A dark stain began to spread around the box – a powerful liquid accelerant intended to boost and spread the fire. The smoke thickened and suddenly there were red flames in the darkness. The flames surged out, burning fiercely.

○

A second box ignited in the canteen, sending spirals of smoke up, lighting the gloom with tongues of fire. Trails of accelerant ran along the floor. Flames followed rapidly.

○

Another box lay alongside the stairway of the upper floor. The flames blackened the doors as they spread and climbed. The floor was soon ablaze. The fire flared up with wild energy.

○

There was a small service room on the ground floor of the tower. A maintenance hatch lay on the floor, exposing the inner workings of the alarm system. The wires had been severed. The water supply to the sprinkler system had been turned off.

Ian Dowd had been busy.

✪

Jack Cooper sat propped against the wall in his office. The computer was still on – screensaver stars flowing endlessly. He was watching them with crazed concentration, his eyes bulging, sweat pouring off his face.

He had no idea of where he was, nor of what was happening to him – all he could focus on was those constantly moving points of white light. It seemed as if the stars were still and he and the room were rushing headlong forwards.

A grey blur floated between him and the stars. There was an acrid smell. He summoned all his strength and managed to tip his head forwards, focusing his eyes under the desk. He watched the dance of the red flames as they spread along the tendrils of spilled liquid.

. One thin line of fire was snaking towards him.

A crack of awareness opened up in his brain. He saw an image of his daughter – far, far away, but calling to him, beckoning him.

He fought to speak. "Maddie," he whispered.

He sweated as he tried to regain control of his body. He dragged himself centimetre by centimetre away from the flames, his legs stretching uselessly behind him as he used his arms to pull himself towards the doorway.

The effort made the room spin around him. The flames had caught the carpet and the desk. The roar of the fire was deafening. The acrid stench stung his nose and throat. The light was blinding.

He was almost at the door. He tried to lift himself on one arm – his other hand reaching up for the door handle. His fingers stretched out but the handle seemed to move further away.

With an agonised gasp, Jack Cooper fell on to his face on the floor and lay still.

He caught a fleeting glimpse of Maddie waving goodbye, before her ghostly shape slipped into the darkness.

Chapter Twenty⊕one

The silver Ducati sped the wrong way along Tottenham Court Road, cutting a dangerous path through the late-night traffic. Alex leant on the throttle, expertly threading his way down the wind-whipped street.

The tall white block of Centre Point came into view.

He felt Maddie's arms tighten around his waist. He heard her shout something, but the rush of air blew her words away.

Alex's eyes narrowed as he approached St Giles Circus. The lights were just changing. He opened up the engine and sped over the crossing. He slowed, bumping the front wheel up over the far kerb. The bike slewed to a standstill on the forecourt.

Maddie scrambled off and ran towards the main entrance of the tower. Alex pulled off his helmet, preparing to follow her.

But something caught his eye.

A parked car under the lee of the high building – two wheels up on the pavement. There was a man at the wheel. Alex took a few steps towards the car – some instinct telling him to be wary.

The man looked up. His eyes gleamed.

Alex breathed a single word. "Dowd!"

The car headlights blazed out. The engine roared into life. A moment later the car was in motion – speeding straight at Alex.

He leapt to one side but the front fender clipped his heel as the car sped past. Alex executed a perfect roll and was up on his feet again.

The car came down off the pavement and shot out across the road. It turned sharply in a screech of brakes and headed along New Oxford Street.

Alex ran to his motorbike. He leapt aboard and kicked the motor back into life.

Dowd was not going to get away from him.

✪

Maddie ran into the building. The security guard was missing from his desk.

Not good.

She ran through the security arch. A figure lay huddled behind the desk. It was the night guard – bound and gagged. She pulled the gag free.

"I was jumped," gasped the man. "He went up – but he's just come back down." Maddie worked on loosening the chords that bound his wrists and ankles.

"It's OK. I know who it was," she said. "Call an ambulance, fast. I think something has happened to my father."

She helped the man to his feet. "Are you OK?" she asked.

He nodded. "I'll come up with you."

"No. Just get help." Maddie ran for the lifts and hammered her hand down on the call pad. She let out a gasp of relief as a pair of doors slid open.

She pressed for the top. The doors closed and the lift began to rise.

"Come on!" she hissed, punching the top button in her frustration. "Move!"

Her father could be injured – dying. The lift seemed to be crawling up through the floors.

Maddie beat her hands on the metal walls, staring at

the floor indicator as it slowly changed.

The lift came to a juddering halt at the top floor. Maddie pushed her way out while the door was still opening. She was hit by a blast of heat and a wall of leaping flame. She was aware of the lift doors closing behind her as she threw her arms up over her face.

The lifts at Centre Point had a built-in failsafe. When the sensors detected a fire, all the lifts descended to the ground floor and immobilised themselves.

Maddie drew back from the fire, hugging the wall as she sought a way forward – unaware that her main line of retreat had been closed off to her.

The entrance to the emergency stairs was in flames.

There was no way down.

✪

Alex's Ducati sped along in the wake of Dowd's car. He leant forwards, his eyes fixed on the tail lights. He was determined not to be thrown off track.

Dowd was driving like a madman, bulldozing his way along the street – forcing other cars to veer off to the sides and sending pedestrians leaping for their lives.

The car bolted across the northern end of Shaftesbury Avenue. It clipped the back of another car, sending it into a spin. Sparks flew. Alex increased his speed – he had to stop this before Dowd killed someone.

They hurtled into Bloomsbury Way. Alex was drawing up level. He could try to force Dowd into the kerb, but if he just kept on going, Alex and the Ducati would go straight under his wheels. It might stop the car, but it would be suicide.

Gradually, Alex edged towards the front of the car. They were racing parallel now, only centimetres separating Alex's knee from the car's side panels.

Alex glanced sideways and saw Dowd's face. His mouth was fixed in a grin of cold rage.

Alex guessed Dowd's intentions a split second before it happened. He slammed on the brakes as Dowd wrenched the wheel to the right. The car careered across Alex's path.

If Alex hit the side of the car at that speed, the impact would kill him.

✪

Maddie gathered herself, pressing her hands against the wall, taking deep breaths. She counted in her head. Three – two – one –

She jumped through the flames and hit the floor running, the heat and smoke swirling around her. Now she could see her target – her father's office a little way along the corridor. Smoke was seeping out.

Maddie pushed at the door. It opened a few

centimetres and then hit against something. A gush of smoke forced her back.

She gulped in clearer air before making a second attempt to get the door open.

She thrust her shoulder against it and managed to force a gap just big enough to edge through.

The room was dark save for the clouded beam of the halogen desk lamp and the hazy glow of the computer screen. Flames leapt through the dense smoke.

Maddie fell to her knees. The air was clearer at floor level. Then she saw her father. He was only a few feet away, lying on his face on the floor. Not moving.

She crawled over and managed to turn him on to his side. She could hear the rasp of his breathing.

Maddie grasped his shirt in both hands and pushed him out of the way of the door. She opened it, then took hold of Jack Cooper's inert body, grabbing him under his arms.

"Come on... Dad..." she gasped. But smoke filled her lungs and she fell into a fit of wracking coughs. The fire was drawing closer. The heat stung her face and hands. Flames were dangerously close to her father's legs.

Maddie renewed her grip on him and hauled backwards, but he was a dead weight. She flexed her muscles, pulling with all her strength.

It was working. She edged through the doorway until his head and shoulders were in the corridor. Smoke was pouring from the room. Maddie got to her feet. She straddled his back, stooped and forced her arms in under him. She heaved, stumbling forwards with spread, unbalanced legs.

Finally she managed to drag him over the threshold. She pulled his feet clear of the doorway. Panting and gasping – her throat raw and her eyes flooding – she reached into the intense heat of the burning office and heaved the door shut.

She knelt, lifting her father's head up on to her lap. This looked bad. She tried to wipe the sweat and grime off his face. His eyes opened slowly. They swam for a few moments and then focused on her face.

"Why aren't... you at the... raid?" he murmured.

"I came back for you," Maddie gasped.

"I was watching the stars..."

"Dad, listen to me, please," Maddie said, trying to keep the panic out of her voice. "We have to get out of here. You have to help me." His eyes lost their grip on her face and he stared glazedly around. "Dad? Did you hear me?"

"Maddie?"

"Yes, I'm here."

"I feel... strange... Maddie..."

A trip hammer came down in her head. Her father had been drugged. Dowd had somehow fed him something to incapacitate him, and then left him to die in his burning office.

She stroked her father's hair, the fear rising in her throat. She stared around. Flames leapt to ceiling height at one end of the corridor, blocking her way down to safety. There was no exit in the other direction – no way down.

Her father muttered incoherently. Smoke billowed from under the door of his office. It stung her eyes. Tears were pouring down her face.

The ceiling tiles began to burn. The carpet was smouldering only half a metre from where she knelt, cradling her father.

"It's OK, Dad," she whispered. "I'll get us out of here. Don't worry." She winced as a tongue of fire flicked out towards them.

There was no way out.

✪

Alex had seen the danger in time to save himself. Instead of ramming straight into the side of the bike, as Dowd had intended, Alex's sudden deceleration meant the car passed right in front of him. Alex tipped the handlebars to the left and narrowly avoided slamming into the back of the car as it hurtled across his path.

Now it was Dowd's turn to find himself in danger.

He had miscalculated, bringing the car in too tight a curve for the speed at which it was travelling.

The car flipped over.

A terrible metallic screech rang out as the car rolled. Fragments of glass flew. Sparks erupted. Pieces of metal were thrown up, and with them shreds of rubber.

The car hammered into the roadway, coming to a halt on its roof.

Alex brought his motorbike to a stop. He jumped off and sprinted back along the road.

He saw petrol leaking. The headlights of the car were still blazing out. Dowd was still in the car.

A huge explosion sent Alex sprawling on his back in the road. A stray spark had ignited the fuel spilling from the ruptured petrol tank.

The car disappeared in a raging ball of fire.

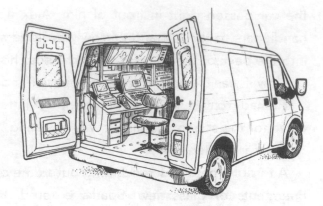

Chapter Twenty•two

Maddie pulled her father away from the spreading flames. The ceiling was a seething mass of smoke. Painful tears were running down her soot-grimed face. She was finding it increasingly difficult to catch her breath. Her throat hurt. There was a bitter taste in her mouth and an acrid smell in her nostrils.

She crouched, keeping down, trying to form coherent thoughts through the panic that was threatening to engulf her. The way to the lift and the emergency stairs was blocked. If they retreated into an office, it would buy them some time, but it would also mean that they would be trapped beyond any hope of rescue. The fire would finish them at its leisure.

Maddie looked at her father. He was staring up with unseeing eyes. His lips were moving, but she couldn't understand anything of what he was saying.

She had to do this on her own.

There was only one chance.

If she could do it.

At the far end of the corridor was a doorway. It led directly to a stairway that would take her to the roof. If she could somehow get her father up there, she might be able to call for help. A helicopter, maybe, could airlift them to safety before the fire broke through.

Maddie ran along the corridor.

The door was unlocked. She dragged it open and scrambled up the stairs.

The door to the roof had a locking bar. She hammered down on it and thrust the door open.

She looked up into the darkness of the sky and breathed clear night air.

Smoke seeped up the stairwell.

Maddie ran back down to her father. She crashed down on to her knees at his side. "Dad?" She slapped his face, trying to get his attention. He looked at her for a moment.

"Hello, Maddie..." he whispered, his voice hoarse

from the smoke. "I thought you'd gone."

She shook him. "No! Don't say that. I'm right here. I'm not going anywhere without you." She had to pause to cough. "I need you to help me, Dad. I need you to sit up and put your arms around my neck. Can you do that for me?"

It was a nightmare in slow motion. Her father was hardly able to control his movements. The dead weight of his legs dragged at him.

The flames roared and crackled. Maddie felt a terrible heat beating on her back. She didn't look around. She didn't want to know how close the fire had come. Smoke shrouded them, filling their lungs, weakening them.

Maddie made a supreme, adrenaline-fuelled effort. Somehow she found the strength to get her father into the fireman's lift position across her shoulders. She held him there with her hands, steadying herself as she knelt, adjusting her balance.

She only had one chance to do this.

She flexed her back and slowly tried to stand. Pain flared through her damaged hip joint.

A voice roared in her head, "I can't do this!"

But then she was on her feet, bowed low under her father's weight. She took a step forwards and didn't fall. The sweat was dripping off her face. The intense heat made her shoes stick to the carpet.

She began the slow, impossible walk to the stairwell. Every few steps she had to stop to regain her balance. Every muscle in her body ached with the effort.

"I can do this. I can." She heard the agonised voice almost without realising that the words were coming from her own mouth.

The stairs were now in front of her. She lifted one foot on to the first step, then shifted her balance and pushed upwards. Her trailing foot came up on to the stair.

It *was* possible. She *could* do it.

It felt to Maddie as if her body was being tested beyond its natural limits. The fight with Tara had left her weak and aching, and now she had to force her bent back to support her father's inert weight – to steel her shaking limbs to carry him to safety.

Finally she fell on the top step, slashing a ragged cut in her knee on the metal threshold of the outer door. The pain cleared her mind. She ducked her head and let her father roll off her back, then she stumbled back down the stairs and wrenched the door shut in the face of the fire.

Maddie hobbled back up, her knee bleeding freely. She eased her father out of the way and hurled the outer door closed. She fell against it, sucking in fresh air. It felt cold up here after the stifling heat of the stairwell. Her whole body was shaking with fear and exhaustion.

Supporting herself on the doorframe, she forced her legs to straighten. Now she could get help. She felt for her mobile phone – but it was gone. Maddie let out a cry of frustration. It must have fallen from her pocket somewhere back down there. It was lost in the inferno on the other side of the door – she would have to rely on Alex.

She checked on her father's condition. He seemed to have slipped into a deeper level of unconsciousness. That was good. If they died up there together, at least he would know nothing about it.

She examined the wound to her knee. The pain was intense. She had nothing to bind it.

Scanning the roofscape, Maddie saw the slender metal crane that supported the mobile maintenance cradle. The cradle itself was about one metre by three with high protective rails. Window cleaners used it – winching themselves up and down the sheer face of the building.

An image came into her mind from some months ago. Repairs were being undertaken on the roof. The cradle had been taken right down to ground level and supplies had been packed into it. Quicker than taking them all the way through reception and up in the lifts.

Maddie limped to the edge of the roof. It was a dizzying drop. Way below her, the cars and taxis looked like playthings on a toy road. An idea was forming in her mind.

The crane stood on solid steel rails that allowed it to be tracked to and fro across the roof. Attached to the base of the winch was a locked metal service box. There was no key, but Maddie was way beyond allowing something like that to stop her.

She found a discarded piece of steel piping and beat at the box's lock until the hatch fell open. There were simple instructions on a laminated board. There was a lever. A green button and a protected red button. She yanked the lever into the ON position and pressed the red button. A faint hum indicated that the thing was now live.

The way on to the cradle was via a narrow walkway of moveable safety bars. There was an operating panel in the cradle. If she could get her father into the cradle, she should be able to lower them down to the ground.

It had to be worth a try.

Maddie went back to her father. She knelt at his head and lifted his shoulders off the ground. Memories crowded her mind as she looked down into his face. All her life, she had relied on him – like a rock she could cling to when things got bad. His strength had helped her get through the death of her mother. He was the role model for everything she liked about herself. And now he was helpless.

"I am going to get us out of here, Dad," she said.

She ignored the agony in her body. Acting on sheer willpower and determination, she dragged her father across the roof and rolled him into the cradle.

She laid him gently on the floor, then stood to lock the safety bars into place.

Maddie stared down at the control panel, trying to clear her head. Another red button and another green button – power on and power off. A lever to control the rate of descent. A warning sign: 'Hard hats *must* be worn.' She almost smiled. "I think I'll risk it just this once," she murmured. She pressed the green button. An amber light ignited on the panel.

She looked down at her father. "OK, Dad, this is it. Keep your fingers crossed."

She gripped the lever and turned it. The cradle rattled and began a slow descent.

Maddie leant heavily on the side bars, taking the weight off her injured knee. Just a few minutes and they'd be on the ground.

The cradle moved smoothly down on its extending

cables, passing down the face of the building. Suddenly, Maddie found herself staring into an office filled with fire. Thick black smoke pressed against the glass.

They came down until they were directly opposite the window. Red tongues licked the glass. There was a loud crack. Maddie's head jerked back in fear.

The heat had snapped the pane of glass from side to side. But it still held – for a few moments at least. She shivered and turned the lever further to speed their descent.

Maddie was aware of a movement at her feet. She looked down. Her father's wild-eyed face was staring up at her. He grabbed her leg and pulled at her.

"Dad! Don't!" Pain blazed in her wounded knee.

Her father's hands clawed at her, dragging her away from the control panel. She stumbled, her fingers slipping from the lever. The moment she let go, the lever snapped into fail-safe and the cradle halted.

Maddie fell to the floor of the cradle. Her father was shouting incoherently, clinging on to her, holding her down.

The serotonin stripper in the Gems had kicked in – her father was wild and crazed – he had no idea of what he was doing. Like a drowning man pulling his rescuer under the water, he fought with Maddie and prevented

205

her from getting back to the control panel.

The cradle rocked perilously on its cables. The derricks creaked under the abnormal strain. Smoke and fire billowed against the cracked window. It could only be moments before the glass shattered and the fire surged out to engulf them.

✖

Camden Lock.

Danny stood by the front entrance of Unit 17.

Operation Flatline was just about finished.

An agent was inside, making a video of the laboratory. It had been a clean and efficient criminal industry. The basic chemicals were stock-piled in cardboard boxes at the far end of the unit. At the other end, the Gems were in hundreds of plastic bags ready to be distributed. In between stood the laboratory equipment needed to synthesise the little pink pills.

"Smart guys," Danny murmured. He grinned. "But not quite smart enough."

The six suspects were in the back of a police van, speeding towards the cells. A couple of agents were loading the contraband into another van, ready to be shipped off for analysis.

Ledger books had been found, detailing payments, couriers and major dealers. Those people would be getting some unwelcome callers in the next few days.

Danny headed back to the MSU. He smiled to himself. This had been a great night. PIC had finally come good. Only one thing puzzled him – where were Alex and Maddie?

His mobile chimed. He flipped it open. "Yeah?"

It was Alex. "Danny – we've got trouble. I'm at Control. There's a fire. Maddie and the boss are trapped in there."

Danny reeled in shock. "What about Tara?" he asked. "Isn't she there?"

"No. Are you still at the unit?"

"Yes."

"OK. You'll find Tara on the other side of the road – she's in an alley. Go find her and put the cuffs on her. If she's awake, watch yourself – she's gone rogue."

"Say that again?" Danny gasped, his mind racing with questions.

"I'll explain later," Alex said. "Just get her into custody, Danny. And tell Randal what's going down over here – he's in command till we know for sure that the boss is OK."

"Was the fire an accident?"

"No. It was Dowd. He's dead." Alex's voice cracked for a moment. "Things look real bad, Danny. The whole of the top floor of the building is on fire. I don't know if they're going to make it."

☒

Maddie stopped struggling – her father's paranoia-fuelled attack was too much for her. She had no strength left to fight him. He was holding her down – panting – moaning – uncontrollable.

She became still in his arms, listening to the rasp of his breath.

"Dad?" she said. "I need you to let go of me, please."

"You'll leave me – just like your mother did..."

It hardly sounded like his voice. Maddie fought down her horror. "No, Dad," she said, managing to keep her voice calm. "I won't leave you. I promise. Look. Let me go – I'll hold your hand. It'll be fine – just let me get up."

Her father's grip relaxed. Maddie sat up. She took hold of his hand. He gripped her fingers tightly. She knelt in the cradle, ignoring the pain in her knee. The flames were beating against the window. There was another crack – but still the glass held. She could just reach the lever. She turned it.

The cradle shuddered and then slowly began again to creep down the tower.

☒

A fire engine had arrived at the scene of the car crash in

Bloomsbury Way. The flames had been extinguished. The car was a blackened hulk. The body was still in there. There was nothing that Alex could do.

He'd sped back to Centre Point. The security guard told him what had happened. Maddie had gone up the tower alone. And now the lifts weren't operating. That could only mean one of two things – either the power had cut out or there was a fire raging up there.

Alex hadn't hesitated. He'd pounded up the stairs – desperate to get to Maddie.

Near the top of the building, he'd begun to smell smoke. Another two flights and he'd heard the crackling of the flames. A final flight and he was staring up at the fire.

There was no way through – no way for him to get up to Maddie. As he'd run back down, he'd taken out his mobile and pressed for Danny.

The police had arrived now. They'd blocked the roads, keeping people back, diverting the traffic and trying to maintain order.

Alex stood in the middle of St Giles Circus, staring up at the white tower of Centre Point.

Maddie was up there – and there was nothing he could do.

Three fire engines came punching along Oxford

209

Street, sirens wailing, lights flashing. The police let them through and they stopped at the foot of the tower. There was little sign from ground level of the blaze that had taken hold of the upper floors. It was too dark to see the smoke that was now pouring from the air vents on the roof.

Alex ran towards the fire engines. The commander was marshalling his troops.

"How many people in there?" he asked Alex.

"Two for certain," said Alex. "The stairs are blocked."

The commander nodded. He sent a team into the building.

Alex stepped back, staring up the rearing white walls – hoping against hope that Maddie and her father were somehow still alive.

Something caught his attention on the far face of the tower. A slender black shape against the concrete and glass. He stared up at it. It was moving – slowly descending – already more than half way down the building.

Alex realised what it was and hope leapt in him. He ran towards the side of the building.

"Come on Maddie," he urged, as he watched the long black shape gliding slowly down towards him. "You can do it."

The cradle drew closer. He shouted out. "Maddie! You're almost there!" It was now only ten floors above him. He couldn't see anyone yet – but it had to be her.

"Maddie!" he shouted.

"Alex!" came a faint voice.

He let out a yell of relief. The cables were almost fully extended. The cradle was swaying as it came down.

Alex stepped back, catching hold of the cradle to steady it as it dropped into reach. He saw Maddie's smoke-grimed face over the edge.

"Get an ambulance," she said, her voice hoarse and cracked. "Dad's not good."

"There's one on the way," Alex said. "Are you OK?"

"I don't know," Maddie said. "Help me with Dad."

Between them they got Jack Cooper out of the cradle and put him into the recovery position. He was ominously still. Maddie fell to the ground at his side, her arms protectively over him, her head on his shoulder.

Alex saw the blood that saturated her leg.

"That looks nasty," he said.

"It doesn't matter," she gasped. She hugged her father. "We did it, Dad. I got us down. Everything's going to be fine."

The wail of an ambulance sounded – growing rapidly closer.

211

Alex rested his hand on Maddie's matted and tangled hair.

Her ordeal was over.

Chapter Twenty•three

PIC Control.

Saturday morning.

11:35.

Ian Dowd's incendiary devices had caused a lot of damage to the offices and corridors on the upper floors of PIC Control, but the firefighters had managed to contain the blaze and get it under control before any structural damage was done to the building. Within two hours, it had all been over. But where the fire had not caused havoc, the chemical foam that the firefighters had used to beat the flames back had left a residue that it would take days to clear up.

A small team of PIC Personnel were making a tour of the wreckage of Control – Jack Cooper, DCIs Baxendale and Randal, Alex, Danny and Maddie, plus a few others and one outsider: Kathryn Grant. Most of the windows had shattered in the heat. The stench of the burning still hung thickly in the air. All of their furniture and equipment had been severely damaged by the smoke.

Maddie pushed her father's new wheelchair across the floor of the open-plan office, crunching through the broken glass and debris, acutely aware that she was performing a task always previously undertaken by Tara Moon.

Maddie's knee had been attended to – it was a wide cut, but not dangerous. A few stitches and a bandage wrap had been all that was needed. That and a few days bed rest. Some chance!

Jack Cooper had discharged himself from hospital first thing that morning. The doctors had protested, but Maddie had understood his need to get back to Control and see for himself just how bad things were.

"Could be worse, boss," Danny said as he gazed around at the mess. "The coffee machine is still in one piece."

Jack Cooper looked at him, one eyebrow raised.

Alex came down from an inspection of the top floor. The stairways had been cleared and the stairs declared safe. "It's not nice up there," he said. He looked at Jack Cooper. "Your office is completely burnt out – there's nothing salvageable in there."

Kathryn Grant was gathering a few sooty documents from Maddie's desk and putting them into a wide black briefcase.

Maddie wheeled her father over to her. "Are your investigations complete, Miss Grant?" he asked.

"I think they are," she said. "Once you told me about Tara Moon's role in all this, it didn't take me long to find what I had been looking for. Miss Moon had a secret bank account where she kept all the money she stole from the department. I imagine her game plan was to take as much as she could and then get herself and Dowd out of the country before she was found out. She didn't quite make it, though."

"Can someone tell me what's going on?" Danny asked. He looked at Kathryn Grant. "What exactly have you been doing here?"

She glanced at Jack Cooper. He nodded.

"I'm a fraud investigator from the National Audit Office," she said. "The Home Secretary asked me to investigate certain financial irregularities which have been showing up in the funding of this department over the past few months."

"What kind of irregularities?" Maddie asked.

"Large amounts of money were going missing," Kathryn Grant said. "I was told to check for signs of embezzlement."

Susan Baxendale looked at Jack Cooper. "I take it you knew all about this?" she asked.

"I did," he said. "And I agreed to give Miss Grant my full co-operation."

"Don't you think the Section Heads might have been informed?" Susan Baxendale said.

Jack Cooper looked at her. "The likelihood was that the thief was at the top of the organisation," he said quietly. "It might have been you, Susan. Especially as you were having secret meetings with Chief Inspector Andrew Blake of Special Branch recruitment."

Susan Baxendale wasn't able to hide her look of surprise.

Jack Cooper looked keenly at her. "Not much happens around here that I don't know about, Susan. Not usually, anyway." He frowned. "Did you get the job?"

Susan Baxendale lifted her chin. "I was offered a post in Special Branch, yes. But I turned it down. I thought it over and I decided I'd rather stay in PIC. If that's OK with you, boss?"

Jack Cooper smiled. "I wouldn't have it any other way."

"Excuse me," Danny said. "This is all very fine and good, and I can't begin to tell you how pleased I am that DCI Baxendale is staying, but I still don't get the deal with Tara. I mean – she was one of us. What the heck went wrong?"

"Ian Dowd went wrong," said Maddie.

"Tara was Dowd's girlfriend," Jack Cooper said. "They had been together for over a year. She kept it quiet at first because she didn't want me to know she had such a strong link with another police department. It became even more important for her to keep her relationship with Dowd a secret when she learnt that he was dealing drugs."

"You mean she knew about his racket and didn't say anything?" said Alex. He let out a long, low whistle.

"None of us suspected her," Jack Cooper said. "Things began to go wrong for her when Dowd was sacked. They knew it was only a matter of time before Internal Affairs would be on his trail. And if they found him – they'd certainly find her. So she stepped up her thieving from a few hundred pounds a week to a few thousand." He looked at Kathryn Grant. "Do we know the full amount?"

"I'm still checking," she said. "But it will come to over a hundred thousand pounds in total."

"I still can't quite believe it," Maddie said. "How could Tara do this to us?"

"She was given a choice," Jack Cooper said. "She made the wrong one. She collapsed when she was told that Dowd was dead. When she recovered, she made a full confession. Dowd must have had a massive influence over her. If not for him..." He paused, his forehead creasing. "But that's something we'll never know. She was working with Dowd all down the line. Dowd wanted revenge – he wanted to see PIC destroyed, and me along with it. He framed Maddie and then he killed Paul Gilmore when he found out that the boy had switched sides. He paid our best contacts to give us false information. It was all intended to undermine us – to make us suffer."

"Did Tara slip us the computer virus?" Danny asked.

Jack Cooper nodded. "That was to humiliate me and to help cover her tracks by destroying our accounts files. But the bottom line was – Dowd wanted me dead."

"There never was an attacker in Paul's flat," Maddie said suddenly. "It was Tara who hit me." Her eyes widened. "She must have injured her own face. Can you imagine the kind of person who could do that to themselves?" She shivered. "And all because of that monster."

"If that's what being in love does to you," Danny murmured. "Count me out!"

Jack Cooper smiled wryly. "My humiliation was meant to be completed by the email Dowd sent to the Home Secretary. It was supposed to be a confession and suicide note combined."

"Fortunately, Margaret Churchill didn't get to see it until this morning," said Kevin Randal, "by which time she already knew what had happened."

Jack Cooper's mobile phone rang. He drew it out.

He stared for a few moments at the name of the caller on the display screen. His eyebrows rose.

He pressed to receive the call.

"Yes, Home Secretary. Good morning. Yes, thank you. The doctors did a good job. I'm fine." There was a pause. "Yes. I'm here right now with some of my people. We're assessing the damage. Yes, considerable, I should think." Another pause. "Yes, I appreciate that."

Maddie looked at Danny and Alex. Her father's face gave nothing away. What was he being told?

"No, I'm sure that's not the case," said Jack Cooper.

"I understand perfectly, Home Secretary. It won't be a problem. Goodbye."

He lowered the phone. He sat there, staring thoughtfully at nothing.

"Dad?" Maddie asked softly. "What was that all about?"

"Hmm?" He looked up at her. "I'm sorry – I've been given a lot of food for thought."

"Boss!" said Danny. "Cut to the chase! Do we clean up or do we clear out?"

Jack Cooper looked at him. "I have just been informed that the Home Secretary has reinstated Police Investigation Command as of eleven o'clock this morning," he said. "She has also agreed a funding package that will allow us to get back on our feet in the shortest possible time." For a moment, it almost looked as thought he was going to smile. "So, Agent Bell, the answer to your question is – start clearing up. Right now."

Danny gazed around at the devastated offices. "Anyone got a feather duster?" he asked.

✪

The three trainees were at Maddie's desk. It was near the emergency exit and had suffered badly in the fire.

Kathryn Grant was putting a few last papers into her briefcase.

"You can have your desk back now," she said to Maddie.

Maddie stared at the charred mess. "Thanks a lot," she said. Grant locked her briefcase and walked away without a backward glance. Maddie glared at her – irritated by the woman's unyielding arrogance.

"Excuse me," Maddie called after her. "Haven't you ever heard of leaving things the way you'd like to find them?"

Kathryn looked over her shoulder, her face deadpan. "I'm sure you can sort it out," she said. "You seem quite capable of clearing up serious messes."

She stepped into the lift and the doors closed on her back.

"She cracked a joke," Danny said with a grin. "She is human after all."

"Just about," said Alex. He looked at Maddie's work space. "Do you want to share with me for the time being?" he asked.

"No," Maddie said. "I'd rather be here, thanks." She banged some dust out of her chair with her fist and then sat down. "This is where I belong."

✪

Centre Point.

On the roof.

17:42.

Maddie, Danny and Alex were taking a short break up on the roof of the building. It was good to get away from the bad smell down there – good to breathe fresh air and feel the wind on their faces.

It had been a hard day for the agents of Police Investigation Command. Their orders were to move everything they could to alternative offices in New Scotland Yard – they would operate from there until Control had been fixed up. It had not been easy.

Maddie was leaning on the parapet, gazing out across London. "I could have died up here," she said thoughtfully.

Danny stood on one side of her and Alex on the other, gazing down at the vibrant city streets.

Maddie frowned. "But we have to carry on, don't we? Even though it's dangerous – this isn't a job we can just turn our backs on."

Alex looked at her. "You sound just like your father," he said.

Maddie stared out over the rooftops of London. She thought of Jack Cooper's unshakeable conviction that what they were doing really mattered. When she spoke again her voice was strong and steady.

"Is that such a bad thing?" she asked.